The Historian's Craft

Marc Bloch

AAKAR

The Historian's Craft
Marc Bloch

First Indian Edition 2017
Reprinted 2018, 2019, 2021, 2022, 2024
Reprinted 2025

ISBN 978-93-5002-466-9

Published by
AAKAR BOOKS
28 E Pocket IV, Mayur Vihar Phase I
Delhi 110 091, India
www.aakarbooks.com

Printed at
D.K. Fine Art Press, Delhi

The Historian's Craft

TO
LUCIEN FEBVRE
BY WAY OF A DEDICATION

IF THIS BOOK should one day be published—if, begun as a simple antidote by which, amid sorrows and anxieties both personal and collective, I seek a little peace of mind, it should turn into a real book, intended to be read—you will find, my friend, another name than yours inscribed upon its dedication page. You can surmise the name this place requires; it is the one permissible allusion to a tenderness too deep and sacred to be spoken. Yet how can I resign myself to seeing you appear in no more than a few chance references? Long have we worked together for a wider and more human history. Today our common task is threatened. Not by our fault. We are vanquished, for a moment, by an unjust destiny. But the time will come, I feel sure, when our collaboration can again be public, and again be free. Meanwhile, it is in these pages filled with your presence that, for my part, our joint work goes on. It will keep what was always its rhythm of fundamental agreement, enlivened, on the surface, by the profitable interplay of our affectionate discussions. Certainly, more than one of the ideas which I propose to uphold I have taken straight from you. With many of the others, I cannot, in honesty, decide whether they are yours, mine, or both of ours. I flatter myself that you will often approve. And you will sometimes rebuke me. In either case, there will be another bond between us.

Fougères,
Creuse,
May 10, 1941

INTRODUCTION

WESTERN MAN has always been historically minded, and this trait has been accentuated during the last two centuries. Laymen are more aware than ever before that they are living and making history—witness the care with which great business organizations are preserving their archives, and the determination of our military authorities to have the history of their commands written "while it is hot." Certainly the number of historians, both professional and amateur, has greatly increased in recent years, as has the quantity of historical writing—quality is another matter. We have histories of games and histories of mail-order houses, histories of diseases and histories of delusions, histories of transportation and histories of highways, as well as the old standard mixtures of political, economic, and social history.

Yet the more history we write the more we worry about the value and nature of history. The increase in the number of books on historiography and historical methodology is proportionally far greater than the increase in the number of historians. Such books have been especially numerous in the last ten or fifteen years, for obvious reasons. We are all asking, as the author of this book asks in his first sentence: "What is the use of history?" What is the use of history, when the values of the past are being ruthlessly discarded? What is the use of history, when we repeat our old errors over and over again? And even if we are sure that history has its uses, are we able to write the kind of history that can be used?

These are the questions that troubled Marc Bloch, as they have troubled so many of his fellow workers. They must have pressed on him with almost unbearable weight in the dark days of 1941, when he began this book. A veteran of the First War, called back to the colors at the age of fifty-three in 1939, he had seen the collapse of France and of everything in which he believed. His Jewish ancestry made it impossible for him to return to his professorship at the Sorbonne; he took refuge first with the exiled University of Strasbourg at Clermont-Ferrand, then with the University of Montpellier. He could have fled to the United States, but he refused to leave France, even the France of Vichy. As he said in his testament, he was so thoroughly French, so impregnated with the spirit and tradition of France, that he did not think he could breathe freely in another country. And if the book was begun under evil auspices it was continued under worse. When the Germans crossed the line of demarcation, after the landings in North Africa, Bloch was driven from academic life. He became a member of the Resistance, a leader of the group centering in Lyons. There he was captured by the Germans in the spring of 1944, imprisoned, and cruelly mistreated. On

June 16, as the Nazi hold on France began to weaken, he was taken from his cell and shot in an open field near Lyons with twenty-six other patriots.

The book was never finished. But, in the large fragment which was completed, we find no bitterness, no discouragement. Bloch kept his serenity, his faith in France, and his belief in the value of history. He used a few of his war experiences, as he used other episodes in his life, to illustrate attitudes and beliefs which he felt were common to many men. But this book is not a product of the war; it is the fruit of the long years of peaceful study and reflection which made him a master of his trade.

As such, it is worth careful study. Not that Bloch was the greatest French historian of his generation, though he would certainly rank high in any list. Not even that he was the most widely read—others excelled in that art of combining exact knowledge with readability which has distinguished French scholarship for many years. His real eminence lay in the fact that he actually put into practice those recommendations for a new kind of history which the profession has been endorsing—and ignoring—for the last fifty years. Others have talked about the narrowness of purely political history, the evils of excessive specialization, and the unreality of the conventional periodization of history —without ever leaving their own limited fields. Bloch not only said that history was a whole, that no period and no topic could be understood except in relation to other periods and topics, but he constantly taught and wrote in accordance with this belief. Though his most important work was in medieval history he gave a course, in his last years of teaching, on the economic development of the United States. Though the Sorbonne listed him as professor of economic history he never made the mistake of assuming that economic factors explain all human behavior. He knew that man is not entirely rational, that society is held together as much by beliefs and customs as by economic interests. He worked constantly for a "wider, more human history," for a history which described how and why people live and work together. He saw life as a whole, as a complicated interplay of ideals and realities, of conscious innovation and unconscious conservation. When he discussed institutions, they were not the petrified fictions of the lawyer, but the changing patterns which emerge from human life. When he discussed ideas, they were not the bloodless, literary abstractions of doctoral dissertations, but the hidden forces which determine behavior and the structure of society. He was capable of infinite attention to detail, but he never forgot that the details had meaning only in the larger framework of the history of human society. All this is illustrated in his fine work on *La société féodale*, a book which is far more than a description of feudal institutions. Throughout the two volumes he sought, above everything else, to understand and explain the state of mind and the habits of life which could produce and support feudal organization.

He was a great practitioner of the new approach to

history in another way, in his ability to discover and use new types of source material. Here again, historians have been preaching for many years that written records are not enough, that we must learn to follow other traces of man's activity in the past, but few historians have taken the trouble to learn how to use these difficult materials. Bloch, in what was probably his greatest book, *Les caractères originaux de l'histoire rurale française,* gave a perfect demonstration of how the job should be done. Old maps, place-names, ancient tools, aerial surveys, folklore—all contributed to his brilliant description of French society during the long centuries when agriculture was the predominant occupation.

These qualities were manifested not only in his books, but in the review *Annales d'histoire économique et sociale,* which he and Lucien Febvre founded in 1929. During the years before the war no other historical periodical had as much influence on the rising generation of scholars. In long review-articles Marc Bloch showed his consuming interest in all aspects of history, his complete freedom from all provinciality, and his generosity in recognizing or even overpraising the contributions of others. In addition, he poured forth an almost inexhaustible store of suggestions for further investigation. If all the books and articles which he called for had been written we should be closer to that history of humanity of which he dreamed.

This book is his testament as a historian—a thoughtful, honest statement by a great craftsman about the principles of his trade. Here he expressed his aims, which were those of most historians of his own and younger generations. Here he set forth his conviction of the unity of all history and of the living connection between present and past which makes history something more than a game for dilettantes. It is unfortunate that he could not finish and polish his work—his style, never easy, is especially difficult in this work and must have given his translator some bad half-hours. But, even incomplete, Bloch has given us a noble statement of the historian's creed, a guide to his fellow workers, and an explanation of the meaning of their work to laymen.

JOSEPH R. STRAYER

A NOTE ON THE MANUSCRIPTS OF THE PRESENT BOOK

by Lucien Febvre

IT is a delicate task, to be undertaken with many scruples, to prepare an unfinished manuscript for publication, especially when even those parts that had been given to the typist would certainly have received a last polishing from the author before going to the printer. But such scruples are outweighed by the satisfaction of making public, even in mutilated form, a notable book.

Marc Bloch long dreamed, as I have done, of putting down his ideas on history in an organized way. I often think, with bitter regret, that while there was yet time we should have collaborated to give our younger generation a kind of new Langlois and Seignobos,[1] to be the manifesto of another generation and the embodiment of an entirely different spirit. It is too late. At any rate, Marc Bloch, when events had deflected him from his path, attempted on his own to realize a plan which we had often discussed together.

I have elsewhere related how, serving as a staff officer in Alsace, and restless under the idleness of the

[1] [*Translator's note: This refers to the famous* Introduction aux Études Historiques, *long used in courses in methodology both in France and in the United States.*]

"phony war," he one day went to a storekeeper at Molsheim and bought a schoolboy's notebook, no doubt just such a one as that in which Henri Pirenne, interned in another village in the heart of Germany in the First War, wrote his history of Europe. On the first page, Bloch wrote a title:

HISTORY OF FRENCH SOCIETY
IN THE STRUCTURE OF EUROPEAN CIVILIZATION.

Somewhat later, he composed the dedication:

To the memory of Henri Pirenne who, at the time his country was fighting beside mine for justice and civilization, wrote in captivity, a history of Europe.

After which, according to his custom, he drafted an introduction: *Reflections for a Reader Interested in Method.* This is followed by a certain number of pages, still in manuscript, constituting a first chapter, entitled: *Birth of France and of Europe.*

The events which Bloch has himself narrated in *The Strange Defeat* put an end to this work. And when, returning to France after the tragic circuit from Dunkerque to London to Brittany, Bloch again set to work, it was to compose the present book. Exactly when did he begin? I cannot say precisely. There is one early date: at the bottom of the moving page which Bloch composed in my honor, we read: "Fougères, Creuse, May 10, 1941." And on a loose sheet, inserted in one of his files, one may also read:

STATE OF WORK: MARCH 11, 1942.

1. Write, in order to finish IV, generalities, civilizations, and read over.
2. Go on to V (change, experience).

After this latter date Bloch did in fact find the time to finish Chapter IV and to begin Chapter V, to which he gave no final title. That was all.

How would Bloch have finished his book? In the papers which have been turned over to me, I have found no orderly plan for the projected work. Or, rather, I have found one but it is anterior to the actual writing, and differs considerably from the plan which he ultimately followed. He there anticipated seven chapters. He entitled them, respectively:

I. Historical Knowledge: Past and Present
II. Historical Observation.
III. Historical Analysis.
IV. Time and History.
V. Historical Experience.
VI. Explanation in History.
VII. The Problem of Prevision.

For a conclusion, Bloch intended to write a study on *The Role of History in Citizenship and Education.* And he expected to devote an appendix to the *Teaching of History.*

The differences between this plan and the work as executed need not be emphasized. If, in general, the substance foreseen for the first five chapters is to be found in the first four chapters of the present book, Bloch would still have had to treat of the problem of chance, of the problem of the individual, of the problem of "determinant" acts or facts; finally, of that problem of prevision to which he would have had to devote an entire chapter. From these indications we can see that we possess over two thirds of the work that he conceived. It may be useful to transcribe here the latter part of the unfinished plan:

VI. EXPLANATION IN HISTORY.

By way of introduction: *the generation of skeptics* (and scientists).

1. *The idea of cause.* The destruction of cause and of motive (the unconscious). Romanticism and spontaneity.
2. *The idea of chance.*
3. The problem of the individual and his differential value. Supplementarily, the epochs, documentarily without individuals. Is history only a science of men in society? Mass history and the elite.
4. *The problem of "determinant" acts or facts.*

VII. THE PROBLEM OF PREVISION.

1. *Prevision, a mental necessity.*
2. *The ordinary errors of prevision.* Economic fluctuations, military history.
3. *The paradox of prevision* in human affairs: prevision which is destroyed by prevision; role of conscious awareness.
4. *Short-term prevision.*
5. *Regularities.*
6. *Hopes and uncertainties.*

The absence of any more precise and detailed notes by Bloch on these last parts of his book is profoundly to be regretted. They would have been reckoned among the most original. Although I well know his ideas—which are mine—on the questions raised by Chapter VII, I believe that we never actually discussed this problem of prevision, which Bloch promised to treat with so much judgment and originality at the end of the work—and which, perhaps, would have been the most strictly original of the whole.

To establish the text of the present book, I have had before me three large files, each a more or less complete copy of the text to be published. These copies are in large part made up of typewritten sheets, amongst which are interspersed manuscript sheets in Marc Bloch's hand, most frequently written upon the back of a first draft which he had crossed out. Essentially, my work as editor has consisted in composing, from these three, one basic copy, complete in all its pages and taking into account all the manuscript corrections which Bloch himself made in the typewritten copy. No addition, no correction, even of mere form, has been supplied to Bloch's text; it is this text, pure and entire, which is to be found printed in this book.

The work was to include references. We have discovered only a few notes, written out in his hand. We have felt no obligation to fill in this gap. A tremendous and not very profitable task, it would have posed insoluble problems at every step.

Let me add that the three copies I mentioned all end in the same way and with the same words: in history, as elsewhere, the causes cannot be assumed. They are to be looked for. . . ."

Finally, and because it is a matter both of dedication and of solemn memory, I cannot but say this:

There was a person to whom Marc Bloch, before departing, would have dedicated one of the great works that we still expected from him. Those of us who knew and loved Marc Bloch were aware of the single-hearted tenderness with which she enveloped him and his children—and of that abnegation with which she had served him as secretary and helped in his labors. I feel it as an obligation which nothing can prevent me from meeting—not even that sense of sentimental reserve which was so strong with Marc Bloch—I feel it as a duty to set down here the name of Madame Marc Bloch, who died in the same cause as her husband and in the same French faith.

TRANSLATOR'S NOTE

I WISH ONLY to remark that, from the outset, the translation of this book has been a co-operative venture, in which my friend and teacher Robert R. Palmer, and my wife, Durinda, have divided the labor equally with me. A further acknowledgment is due Joseph R. Strayer for the many valuable suggestions made in his reading of the manuscript.

PETER PUTNAM

CONTENTS

THE HISTORIAN'S CRAFT

INTRODUCTION

"TELL ME, Daddy. What is the use of history?"

Thus, a few years ago, a young lad in whom I had a very special interest questioned his historian father. I wish I could say of this book that it is my answer. I can conceive no higher praise for a writer than to be able to speak in the same tone to savants and schoolboys alike, but so noble a simplicity is the privilege of the select few. At any rate, this question from a child, whose thirst for knowledge I was not, perhaps, too well able to satisfy at the time, now serves me well as a point of departure. Doubtless there are some who will consider this a naïve approach, but to me it seems entirely to the point.[1] The problem which it poses, with

[1] In which I find myself, from the beginning, in an unlooked-for opposition to the *Introduction aux Études Historiques* of Langlois and Seignobos. The above passage had already been written, when, in the Foreword of the latter (p. xii), I chanced to see a list of "idle questions." There, word for word, appeared the following: "What is the use of history?" It is the same doubtless with this problem as with any problem concerning the *raison d'être* of our thoughts and actions: those minds which by nature are indifferent to them—or have intentionally determined to make themselves so—always find it difficult to understand that other minds find them the subject of absorbing reflections. Nevertheless, since the opportunity is thus offered me, I think it is better immediately to establish my

the embarrassing forthrightness of that implacable age, is no less than that of the legitimacy of history.

Behold, then, the historian called to render his accounts! He does so not without an inner tremor. What craftsman, grown old in his trade, has not asked himself with a sudden qualm whether he has spent his life wisely? The question far transcends the minor scruples of a professional conscience. Indeed, our entire Western civilization is concerned in it.

For, unlike others, our civilization has always been extremely attentive to its past. Everything has inclined it in this direction: both the Christian and the classical heritage. Our first masters, the Greeks and the Romans, were history-writing peoples. Christianity is a religion of historians. Other religious systems have been able to found their beliefs and their rites on a mythology nearly outside human time. For sacred books, the Christians have books of history, and their liturgies commemorate, together with episodes from the terrestrial life of a God, the annals of the church and the lives of the saints. Christianity is historical in

---

position, as regards a book which is justly famous and which mine, arranged upon a different and, in certain of its parts, a much less fully developed plan, does not by any means pretend to replace. I was the pupil of both its authors, and particularly of M. Seignobos. Both showed me valuable tokens of their good will. My education owed a great deal both to their teaching and to their work. But both have not only taught us that the historian's first duty is to be sincere; they fully appreciated that the very progress of our studies is founded upon the inevitable opposition between generations of scholars. Therefore, I shall be keeping faith with their teaching in criticizing them most freely wherever I may deem it useful; just as I hope, some day, that my pupils will criticize me in their turn.

another and, perhaps, even deeper sense. The destiny of humankind, placed between the Fall and the Judgment, appears to its eyes as a long adventure, of which each life, each individual pilgrimage, is in its turn a reflection. It is in time and, therefore, in history that the great drama of Sin and Redemption, the central axis of all Christian thought, is unfolded. Our art, our literary monuments, resound with echoes of the past. Our men of action have its real or pretended lessons incessantly on their lips. Of course, differences of group psychology can be noted. Cournot long ago observed that the French people in the mass, everlastingly inclined to reconstruct the world on lines of reason, live their collective memories much less intensely than the Germans, for example.[2] Without doubt, too, civilizations may change. It is not in itself inconceivable that ours may, one day, turn away from history, and historians would do well to reflect upon this possibility. If they do not take care, there is danger that badly understood history could involve good history in its disrepute. But should we come to this, it would be at the cost of a serious rupture with our most unvarying intellectual traditions.

For the present, our discussion has reached only the

---

[2] The antihistorical Frenchman: Cournot, *Souvenirs*, p. 43, on the subject of the absence of any royalist sentiment at the end of the Empire, remarks: ". . . for the explanation of the singular fact before us, I believe we must also take into account the scant popularity of our history and the underdeveloped consciousness of historical tradition among our lower classes, for reasons too lengthy for analysis."

stage of probing the conscience. And, indeed, whenever our exacting Western society, in the continuing crisis of growth, begins to doubt itself, it asks itself whether it has done well in trying to learn from the past, and whether it has learned rightly. Read what was written before the war, or, for that matter, what might be written today. Among the confused murmurings of the present, you will almost certainly hear this complaint mingling its voice with the others. I myself chanced to overhear its echo in the very heart of the great drama. It was in June 1940—the very day, if I remember aright, of the German entry into Paris. In a Norman garden, stripped of our troops, we of the general staff consumed our idle hours in ruminating over the causes of the disaster. "Are we to believe that history has betrayed us?" one of us cried. So it was that the anguish of a mature man united its bitter accents with the simple curiosity of the boy. Both demand an answer.

"What is the use of history?"

What is here meant by "use"? But, before proceeding to this question, let me insert one word of apology. The circumstances of my present life, the impossibility of reaching any large library, and the loss of my own books have made me dependent upon my notes and upon memory. Both the supplementary reading and the research demanded by the very laws of the craft I here propose to describe have been denied me. Will it, one day, be granted to me to fill in the gaps? Never entirely, I fear. I can therefore only ask indulgence. I should say: "I plead guilty," were it not that, by so doing, I might seem overly presumptuous in assuming responsibility for the evils of destiny.

Certainly, even if history were judged incapable of other uses, its entertainment value would remain in its favor. Or, to be more exact (for everyone seeks his own pleasures), it is incontestable that it appears entertaining to a large number of men. As far back as I can remember, it has been for me a constant source of pleasure. As for all historians, I think. If not, why have they chosen this occupation? To anyone who is not a blockhead, all the sciences are interesting; yet each scholar finds but one that absorbs him. Finding it, in order further to devote himself to it, he terms it his "vocation," his "calling."

This unquestionable fascination of history requires us to pause and reflect.

Its role, both as the germ and, later, as the spur to action, has been and remains paramount. Simple liking precedes the yearning for knowledge. Before the work of science, fully conscious of its ends, comes the instinct which guides it. Our intellectual history abounds in examples of similar origins. Even physics began with cabinets of curiosities, and the elves of antiquarianism have cut capers about the cradle of more than one serious study. Such was the genesis of archæology and, more recently, of folklore. Readers of Alexander Dumas may well be potential historians who lack only training to find the purer and, to my way of thinking, the keener pleasure of true research.

Moreover, this charm will be far from diminished once methodical inquiry, with all its necessary austerities, has begun. On the contrary, all true historians will bear witness that the fascination then gains in both scope and intensity. The same is true of any intellectual discipline, but, of course, history has its peculiar æsthetic pleasures. The spectacle of human activity which forms its particular object is, more than any other, designed to seduce the imagination—above all when, thanks to its remoteness in time or space, it is adorned with the subtle enchantment of the unfamiliar. The great Leibniz himself admitted as much, and, when he turned from abstract speculation on mathematics and theodicy to the deciphering of the ancient charters and chronicles of Imperial Germany, he, like the rest of us, experienced "the thrill of learning singular things." Let us guard against stripping our science of its share of poetry. Let us also beware of the inclination, which I have detected in some, to be ashamed of this poetic quality. It would be sheer folly to suppose that history, because it appeals strongly to the emotions, is less capable of satisfying the intellect.

Nevertheless, were the nearly universal fascination of history its only justification—if it were, in short, only a pleasant pastime, like bridge or fishing—would it be worth all the trouble we take to write it? To write it, I mean, with integrity, with truth, with the utmost possible penetration into its hidden causes, and, hence, with difficulty? Mere amusement, André Gide has written, is no longer permitted us in our day, even, he added, when it is the amusement of the intelligence. That was said in 1938. In 1942, as I write in my turn, how much graver a significance the remark assumes! Surely, in a world which stands upon the threshold of the chemistry of the atom, which is only beginning to fathom the mystery of interstellar space, in this poor world of ours which, however justifiably proud of its science, has created so little happiness for itself, the tedious minutiæ of historical erudition, easily capable of consuming a whole lifetime, would deserve condemnation as an absurd waste of energy, bordering on the criminal, were they to end merely by coating one of our diversions with a thin veneer of truth. Either all minds capable of better employment must be dissuaded from the practice of history, or history must prove its legitimacy as a form of knowledge.

But here a new question arises. What is it, exactly, that constitutes the legitimacy of an intellectual endeavor?

No one today, I believe, would dare to say, with the orthodox positivists, that the value of a line of research is to be measured by its ability to promote action. Experience has surely taught us that it is impossible to decide in advance whether even the most abstract speculations may not eventually prove extraordinarily helpful in practice. It would inflict a strange mutilation upon humanity to deny it a right to appease its intellectual appetites apart from all consideration of its material welfare. Even were history obliged to be eternally indifferent to *homo faber* or to *homo politicus,* it would be sufficiently justified by its necessity for the full flowering of *homo sapiens.* Yet, even with this limitation, the question is not immediately resolved.

The nature of our intelligence is such that it is stimulated far less by the will to know than by the will to understand, and, from this, it results that the only sciences which it admits to be authentic are those which succeed in establishing explanatory relationships between phenomena. The rest is, as Malebranche put it, mere "polymathy." Now, polymathy can well assume the form either of recreation or of mania, but it cannot today, any more than in the time of Malebranche, pass for one of the proper tasks of the intellect. Even apart from any application to conduct, history will rightfully claim its place among those sciences truly worthy of endeavor only in proportion as it promises us, not simply a disjointed and, you might say, a nearly infinite enumeration, but a rational classification and progressive intelligibility.

However, it is undeniable that a science will always seem to us somehow incomplete if it cannot, sooner or later, in one way or another, aid us to live better. Moreover, should we not feel this sentiment with particular force as regards history, so much the more clearly destined to work for the profit of man, in that it has man himself and his actions for its theme? In fact, a long-standing penchant prompts us, almost by instinct, to demand of it the means to direct our actions and, therefore, as in the case of the conquered soldier mentioned above, we become indignant if, perchance, it seems incapable of giving us guidance. The question of the use of history, in the strict and "pragmatic" sense of the word "use," is not to be confounded with that of its strictly intellectual legitimacy. Moreover, this question of use must always come second in the order of things, for, to act reasonably, it is first necessary to understand. Common sense dictates that we no longer avoid this problem.

Certain among our would-be counselors have already given answers to these questions. They have sought to chide our optimism. The most indulgent have said that history is both unprofitable and unsound; others, with a severity which admits of no compromise, that it is pernicious. One of them, and not the least celebrated, has declared it "the most dangerous compound yet contrived by the chemistry of the intellect." These condemnations offer a terrible temptation, in that they justify ignorance in advance. Fortunately for those of us who still retain our intellectual curiosity, there is, perhaps, an appeal from their verdict.

But if the debate is to be revived, it is important that it be based upon more trustworthy data.

For there is one precaution which the ordinary detractors of history seem not to have heeded. Their words lack neither eloquence nor wit, but they have, for the most part, neglected to ask themselves exactly what it is they are discussing. The picture which they have formed for themselves of our studies has not been drawn in the workshop. It savors rather of the debating-platform than of the study. Above all, it is out of date. Therefore, when all is said and done, it may well be that all their energy has been expended only to conjure away a phantom. Our effort here must be very different. The methods whose value and certainty we shall attempt to assess are those actually used in research, right down to the lowly and delicate technical details. Our problems will be the same as those which the historian's material imposes upon him every day. In a word, our primary objective is to explain how and why a historian practices his trade. It will then be the business of the reader to decide whether this trade is worth practicing.

Let us take care, however. Even thus defined and limited, the task is not so simple as it seems. It might be, were we dealing with one of the practical arts which are sufficiently explained when time-tested manual operations are enumerated one after another. But history is neither watchmaking nor cabinet construction. It is an endeavor toward better understanding and, consequently, a thing in movement. To limit oneself to describing a science just as it is will always be to betray it a little. It is still more important to tell how it expects to improve itself in the course of time. Now, such an undertaking inevitably involves a rather large dose of personal opinion. Indeed, every science is continually beset at each stage of its development by diverging tendencies, and it is scarcely possible to decide which is now dominant without prophesying the future. We shall not shirk this obligation. The dread of responsibility is as discreditable in intellectual matters as in any others. But it is only honest to give the reader fair warning.

The more so, as the difficulties which every study of methodology encounters vary greatly according to the point which the particular discipline has reached upon the always irregular curve of its development. For example, fifty years ago, when Newton still reigned supreme, it was far easier than today to frame, with all the precision of a blueprint, a thesis on mechanics. But history is still in that stage which is very indulgent of statements of positive certainties.

For history is not only a science in movement. Like all those which have the human spirit for their object, this newcomer in the field of rational knowledge is also a science in its infancy. Or to explain more fully, having grown old in embryo as mere narrative, for long encumbered with legend, and for still longer preoccupied with only the most obvious events, it is still very young as a rational attempt at analysis. Now, at last, it struggles to penetrate beneath the mere surface of actions, rejecting not only the temptations of legend and rhetoric, but the still more dangerous modern poisons of routine learning and empiricism parading as common sense. In several of the most essential problems of method, it has not passed beyond the first tentative gropings, and that is why Fustel de Coulanges and, even before him, Bayle came very near the truth when they called it "the most difficult of all the sciences."

But is this merely an illusion? However uncertain our road at many points, we are, it seems to me, at the present hour better placed than our predecessors to see a little light on the path ahead.

The generations just prior to our own, in the last decades of the nineteenth century and even in the first years of the twentieth, were as if mesmerized by the Comtian conception of physical science. This hypnotic *schema*, extending to every province of the intellect, seemed to them to prove that no authentic discipline could exist which did not lead, by immediate and irrefutable demonstrations, to the formulation of absolute certainties in the form of sovereign and universal laws. Such was the nearly unanimous opinion at the time, but when applied to historical studies it gave birth, depending upon the temperament of the individual historian, to two opposing schools.

The first believed it really possible and tried their best to establish a science of human evolution which would conform to a sort of pan-scientific ideal. They were willing to abandon, as outside a true science of man, a great many eminently human realities which appeared to them stubbornly insusceptible to rational comprehension. This residue they scornfully called mere events or happenstance. It was also a good part of the most intimate and individual side of life. Such was, in sum, the position of the sociological school founded by Durkheim. (Of course the early rigidity of principle was gradually softened in practice, though reluctantly, by men too intelligent not to yield before the force of things as they are.) To this great scientific effort our studies are vastly indebted. It has taught us to analyze more profoundly, to grasp our problems more firmly, and even, I dare say, to think less shoddily. It will be spoken of here only with infinite gratitude and respect. If it seems sterile now, that is only the price that all intellectual movements must pay, sooner or later, for their moment of fertility.

The other school of inquirers took a quite different point of view. Unsuccessful in cramming the stuff of history into the legalistic framework of physical science, and particularly disturbed, because of their early training, by the difficulties, doubts, and many fresh beginnings required by documentary criticism, they drew from their inquiries the moral lesson of a disillusioned humility. In the final reckoning, they felt that they were devoting their talents to a discipline which promised neither very positive conclusions in the present, nor the hope of progress in the future. They tended to view history less as truly scientific knowledge than as a sort of æsthetic play, a hygienic exercise favorable to health of mind. They have sometimes been called *historiens historisants*, possessing the truly "historical" point of view; but such a judgment does injury to our profession, for it seems to find the essence of history in the very denial of its possibilities. For my part, I should prefer to find a more expressive symbol for them in the moment of French thought with which they are associated.

The amiable and skeptical Sylvestre Bonnard, if we accept the dates which Anatole France's book assigns his doings, is an anachronism, quite like the old saints whom the writers of the middle ages naïvely depicted in the colors of their own time. Sylvestre Bonnard (if we grant that fictitious character a moment of existence in the flesh)—the "real" Sylvestre Bonnard, born under the First Empire—would have belonged to the generation of the romantic historians. He would have shared their stirring and prolific enthusiasms, their ingenuous faith in the future of the "philosophy" of history. Let us pass over the epoch in which he is supposed to have lived. Let us restore him to the period in which his imaginary life was written by Anatole France. He can then be regarded as the patron saint of a whole group of historians, roughly the intellectual contemporaries of his biographer. They were profoundly honest workmen, but a little short-winded. We may compare them to the children of debauched fathers, their constitutions had been weakened by wild historical orgies of romanticism. They felt rather small beside their colleagues in the laboratory; they were more inclined to recommend caution than daring. Even so vigorous an intelligence as that of my beloved teacher, Charles Seignobos, once let fall a saying that may fairly stand as their slogan: "It is useful to ask oneself questions, *but very dangerous to answer them.*" Surely, this is not the remark of a braggart, but where would physics be today if the physicists had shown no greater daring?

Our mental climate has changed. The kinetic theory of gases, Einstein's mechanics, and the quantum theory have profoundly altered that concept of science which, only yesterday, was unanimously accepted. They have not weakened it; they have only made it more flexible. For certainty, they have often substituted the infinitely probable; for the strictly measurable, the notion of the eternal relativity of measurement. Their influence has even affected the countless minds (and, alas, I must number mine among them) which, thanks to defects in intelligence or early training, have been able to follow the great metamorphosis only at a distance and as if by a reflected light. Hence, we are much better prepared to admit that a scholarly discipline may pretend to the dignity of a science without insisting upon Euclidian demonstrations or immutable laws of repetition. We find it far easier to regard certainty and universality as questions of degree. We no longer feel obliged to impose upon every subject of knowledge a uniform intellectual pattern, borrowed from natural science, since, even there, that pattern has ceased to be entirely applicable. We do not yet know what the sciences of man will some day be. We do know that in order to exist—and, it goes without saying, to exist in accordance with the fundamental laws of reason—they need neither disclaim nor feel ashamed of their own distinctive character.

I should like professional historians and, above all, the younger ones to reflect upon these hesitancies, these incessant soul-searchings, of our craft. It will be the surest way they can prepare themselves, by a deliberate choice, to direct their efforts reasonably. I should desire above all to see ever-increasing numbers of them arrive at that broadened and deepened history which some of us—more every day—have begun to conceive. If my book can help them, I shall feel that it was not in vain. I confess that that is, in part, its aim.

But I do not write exclusively, or even chiefly, for the private use of the guild. The uncertainties of our science must not, I think, be hidden from the curiosity of the world. They are our excuse for being. They bring freshness to our studies. Surely we have the right to claim for history the indulgence due to all new ventures. The incomplete, if it is perpetually straining to realize itself, is quite as enticing as the most perfect success. To paraphrase Péguy, the good husbandman takes as much pleasure in plowing and sowing as in the harvest.

It is fitting that these few words of introduction be concluded with a confession. Each science, taken by itself, represents but a fragment of the universal march toward knowledge. I have given an example above; in order to understand and appreciate one's own methods of investigation, however specialized, it is indispensable to see their connection with all simultaneous tendencies in other fields. Now this study of methods for their own sake is, in its turn, a specialized trade, whose technicians are called philosophers. That is a title to which I cannot pretend. Through this gap in my education this essay will doubtless lose much in both precision of language and breadth of horizon. I submit it for what it is and no more: the memorandum of a craftsman who has always liked to reflect over his daily task, the notebook of a journeyman who has long handled the ruler and the level, without imagining himself to be a mathematician.

CHAPTER I

HISTORY, MEN, AND TIME

1. The Choice of the Historian

THE WORD "history" is very old—so old that men have sometimes grown weary of it. It is true that they have rarely gone so far as to wish to erase it from the vocabulary entirely. Even the sociologists of the Durkheim school make room for it. They do so, to be sure, only in order to relegate it to one poor corner of the sciences of man—a sort of secret dungeon in which, having first reserved for sociology all that appears to them susceptible of rational analysis, they shut up the human facts which they condemn as the most superficial and capricious of all.

Here, on the contrary, we shall preserve the broadest interpretation of the word "history." The word places no *a priori* prohibitions in the path of inquiry, which may turn at will toward either the individual or the social, toward momentary convulsions or the most lasting developments. It comprises in itself no credo; it commits us, according to its original meaning, to nothing other than "inquiry." Assuredly, since its first appearance on the lips of men, more than two millenniums ago, its content has changed a great deal. Such is the fate of all truly living terms in a language. If the sciences were obliged to find a new name each time they made an advance—what a multitude of christenings! and what a waste of time for the academic realm!

In remaining quietly loyal to its glorious Hellenic name, our history need be no more like that of Hecatæus of Miletus than the physics of Lord Kelvin or Langevin is like that of Aristotle. What, then, is this history of ours?

At the start, while focusing our attention upon the *real* problems of investigation, it would be pointless to draw up a tedious and inflexible definition. What serious workman has ever burdened himself with such articles of faith? It is not only that their meticulous precision omits the best in every intellectual creation—the half-formed impulse toward a knowledge still undetermined but capable of extension. The worst danger of such careful definitions is that they only bring further limitations. "This subject," declares the Divine Lexicographer, "or that means of treating it, is, no doubt seductive, but—take care, O young apprentice!—it is not history!" Are we then the rules committee of an ancient guild, who codify the tasks permitted to the members of the trade, and who, with a list once and for all complete, unhesitatingly reserve their exercise to the licensed masters? [1] The physicists

[1] [*Translator's note: The following note is only a fragment on a loose sheet. The beginning is lost.*] . . . as Lucien Febvre has pointed out, history itself, when consulted as to the path which the development of mankind has followed, is obliged to contradict them most flagrantly. Not only does each science, taken separately, find its most successful craftsman among the refugees from neighboring

and chemists are wiser—so far as I know, they have never been seen to quarrel about the respective rights of physics, of chemistry, of physical chemistry, or (assuming the existence of such a term) of chemical physics.

It is no less true that, faced with the vast chaos of reality, the historian is necessarily led to carve out that particular area to which his tools apply; hence, to make a selection—and, obviously, not the same as that of the biologist, for example, but that which is the proper selection of the historian. Here we have an authentic problem of action. It will pursue us throughout our study.

2. *History and Men*

It is sometimes said: "History is the science of the past." To me, this is badly put.

For, to begin with, the very idea that the past as such can be the object of science is ridiculous. How, without preliminary distillation, can one make of phenomena, having no other common character than that of being not contemporary with us, the matter of rational knowledge? On the reverse side of the medal, can one imagine a complete science of the universe in its present state?

areas. Pasteur, who renovated biology, was not a biologist—and during his lifetime he was often made to feel it; just as Durkheim, and Vidal de la Blache, the first a philosopher turned sociologist, the second a geographer, were neither of them ranked among the licensed historians, yet they left an incomparably deeper mark upon historical studies at the beginning of the twentieth century than any specialists.

Doubtless, in the origins of historiography, the old annalists were scarcely embarrassed by these scruples. They narrated pell-mell events whose only connection was that they had happened about the same time: eclipses, hailstorms, and the sudden appearance of astonishing meteors along with battles and the deaths of kings and heroes. But into these early reminiscences of humanity, as garbled as the observations of a small child, a sustained effort of analysis has gradually introduced the necessary classification. It is true that our language, fundamentally conservative, freely retains the name of history for any study of a change taking place in time. The custom is harmless, for it deceives no one. In that sense, there is a history of the solar system, because the stars which compose it have not always been as we now see them. It belongs to the province of astronomy. There is a history of volcanic eruptions which is, I am sure, of most lively interest as regards the composition of the earth. It does not concern the history of historians.

Or, at least, it does so only in so far as its observations chance to coincide with the specific preoccupations of our history. How, then, is the division of labor determined in practice? To understand this, a single example will be worth more than a thousand words.

In the tenth century A.D., a deep gulf, the Zwin, indented the Flemish coast. It was later blocked up with sand. To what department of knowledge does the study of this phenomenon belong? At first sight, anyone would suggest geology. The action of alluvial deposit, the operation of ocean currents, or, perhaps, changes in sea level: was not geology invented and put on earth to deal with just such as these? Of course. But at close range, the matter is not quite so simple. Is there not first a question of investigating the origin of the transformation? Immediately, the geologist is forced to ask questions which are no longer strictly within his jurisdiction. For there is no doubt that the silting of the gulf was at least assisted by dyke construction, changing the direction of the channel, and drainage—all activities of man, founded in collective needs and made possible only by a certain social structure. At the other end of the chain there is a new problem: the consequences. At a little distance from the end of the gulf, and communicating with it by a short river passage, rose a town. This was Bruges. By the waters of the Zwin it imported or exported the greatest part of the merchandise which made of it, relatively speaking, the London or New York of that day. Then came, every day more apparent, the advance of the sand. As the water receded, Bruges vainly extended its docks and harbor further toward the mouth of the river. Little by little, its quays fell asleep. To be sure, this was not the sole cause of its decline. (Does the physical ever affect the social, unless its operations have been prepared, abetted, and given scope by other factors which themselves have already derived from man?) But this was certainly at least one of the most efficacious of the links in the causal chain.

Now, the act of a society remodeling the soil upon which it lives in accordance with its needs is, as any one recognizes instinctively, an eminently "historical" event. It is the same with the vicissitudes of a powerful seat of trade. Hence, in an example entirely characteristic of the topography of learning, we see, on the one hand, an area of overlap, where the union of two disciplines is shown to be indispensable to any attempt at explanation; on the other, a point of transition, where when a phenomenon has been described with the sole exception that its consequences remain undetermined, it is, in some definitive way, yielded up by one discipline to another. What is it that seems to dictate the intervention of history? It is the appearance of the human element.

Long ago, indeed, our great forebears, such as Michelet or Fustel de Coulanges, taught us to recognize that the object of history is, by nature, man.[2] Let us say rather, men. Far more than the singular, favoring abstraction, the plural which is the grammatical form of

---

[2] Fustel de Coulanges, opening lecture of 1862, in *Revue de Synthèse historique,* t. II, 1901, p. 243; Michelet, course at the École Normale, 1829, cited by G. Monod, *La Vie et la Pensée de Jules Michelet,* t. I, p. 127: "We are concerned at the same time with the study of the individual man, and that will be philosophy —and with the study of the social man, and that will be history." It is proper to add that, much later, Fustel remarked in a more concise and fuller formula, of which the foregoing exposition is hardly more than a commentary: "History is not the accumulation of events of every kind which happened in the past. It is the science of human societies." But this is, perhaps, to curtail the role of the individual too much in history; man in society, and societies, are not precisely equivalent ideas.

relativity is fitting for the science of change. Behind the features of landscape, behind tools or machinery, behind what appear to be the most formalized written documents, and behind institutions, which seem almost entirely detached from their founders, there are men, and it is men that history seeks to grasp.[3] Failing that, it will be at best but an exercise in erudition. The good historian is like the giant of the fairy tale. He knows that wherever he catches the scent of human flesh, there his quarry lies.

From the character of history as the knowledge of men derives its peculiar situation as regards the problem of expression. Is it "science" or "art"? About 1800, our great-grandfathers delighted in solemn debates on this question. Later, about 1890, saturated with the aura of a rather primitive positivism, the methodologists were indignant that the public should attach an excessive importance to what they called "form" in historical works. Art versus science, form versus matter: the history of scholarship abounds with such fine debates!

There is no less beauty in a precise equation than in a felicitous phrase, but each science has its appropriate æsthetics of language. Human actions are essentially very delicate phenomena, many aspects of which elude mathemathical measurement. Properly to translate them into words and, hence, to fathom

---

[3] "Not man, again, never man. Human societies, organized groups." Lucien Febvre, *La Terre et l'évolution humaine*, p. 201.

them rightly (for can one perfectly understand what he does not know how to express?), great delicacy of language and precise shadings of verbal tone are necessary. Where calculation is impossible we are obliged to employ suggestion. Between the expression of physical and of human realities there is as much difference as between the task of a drill operator and that of a lutemaker: both work down to the last millimeter, but the driller uses precision tools, while the lutemaker is guided primarily by his sensitivity to sound and touch. It would be unwise either for the driller to adopt the empirical methods of the lutemaker or for the lutemaker to imitate the driller. Will anyone deny that one may not feel with words as well as with fingers?

3. Historical Time

We have called history "the science of men." That is still far too vague. It is necessary to add: "of men in time." The historian does not think of the human in the abstract. His thoughts breathe freely the air of the climate of time.

To be sure, it is difficult to imagine that any of the sciences could treat time as a mere abstraction. Yet, for a great number of those who, for their own purposes, chop it up into arbitrarily homogeneous segments, time is nothing more than a measurement. In contrast, historical time is a concrete and living reality with an irreversible onward rush. It is the very plasma in which events are immersed, and the field within which they become intelligible. The number of seconds, years, or centuries required for a radioactive substance to change into other substances is a fundamental datum for the atomic scientist. But the idea any particular one of these metamorphoses had occurred a thousand years ago, or yesterday, or today, or that another such is bound to occur tomorrow—all of which would unquestionably interest the geologist, because geology is, in its way, a historical discipline—leaves the physicist perfectly unmoved. In his turn, no historian would be satisfied to state that Cæsar devoted eight years to the conquest of Gaul, or that it took fifteen years for Luther to change from the orthodox novice of Erfurt into the reformer of Wittenberg. It is of far greater importance to him to assign the conquest of Gaul its exact chronological place amid the vicissitudes of European societies; and, without in the least denying the eternal aspect of such spiritual crises as Brother Martin's, he will feel that he has given a true picture of it only when he has plotted its precise moment upon the life charts of both the man who was its hero and the civilization which was its climate.

Now, this real time is, in essence, a continuum. It is also perpetual change. The great problems of historical inquiry derive from the antitheses of these two attributes. There is one problem especially, which raises the very *raison d'être* of our studies. Let us assume two consecutive periods taken out of the uninterrupted sequence of the ages. To what extent does the connection which the flow of time sets between them predominate, or fail to predominate, over the differences born out of that same flow? Should the knowledge of the earlier period be considered indispensable or superfluous for the understanding of the later?

4. *The Idol of Origins*

It will never be amiss to begin with an acknowledgment of our faults. The explanation of the very recent in terms of the remotest past, naturally attractive to men who have made of this past their chief subject of research, has sometimes dominated our studies to the point of a hypnosis. In its most characteristic aspect, this idol of the historian tribe may be called the obsession with origins. Moreover, in the development of historical thought, it has enjoyed its moment of particular favor. It was Renan, I believe, who once wrote (I quote from memory, therefore, I fear, inexactly): "In all human affairs, it is the origins which deserve study before everything else." And, before him, Sainte-Beuve: "With curiosity, I scrutinize and make note of all beginnings." The idea is entirely typical of their age. So also is the word "origins." Shortly after *The Origins of Christianity* came *The Origins of Contemporary France*. Not to mention mere followers. However, the word "origins" is disturbing, because it is ambiguous.

Does it mean simply "beginnings"? That would be relatively clear—except that for most historical realities the very notion of a starting-point remains singularly elusive. It is doubtless a matter of definition, but of a definition which it is unfortunately all too easy to forget to give.

On the other hand, is "origins" taken to mean the causes? In that case, there will be no difficulties other than those which are always inherent in the nature of causal inquiry (and even more so, no doubt, in the sciences of man.)

But there is a frequent cross-contamination of the two meanings, the more formidable in that it is seldom very clearly recognized. In popular usage, an origin is a beginning which explains. Worse still, a beginning which is a complete explanation. There lies the ambiguity, and there the danger!

Some most interesting researches might be undertaken on that embryogenic obsession which is so marked among exegetes. "I do not understand your agitation," Barrès confessed to a priest who had lost faith. "What have the arguments of a handful of savants about a few Hebrew words to do with my feeling? The atmosphere of a church is quite enough." And Maurras, in his turn: "How do the Gospels of four obscure Jews concern me?" ("Obscure," means, I imagine, plebeian; for, as regards Matthew, Mark, Luke, and John, it would be hard to ignore, at least, a certain literary notoriety). These pranksters are pulling our leg. Neither Pascal nor Bossuet would speak so boldly. Doubtless, a religious experience apart from history is conceivable. For the pure Deist, it is enough to have the inner light to believe in Cod. But not to believe in the God of the Christians. For Christianity, as I have already pointed out, is essentially a historical religion: a religion, that is, whose prime dogmas are based on events. Read over your creed: "I believe in Jesus Christ . . . who was crucified under Pontius Pilate . . . and who rose from the dead on the third day." Here the beginnings of the faith are also its foundations.

Now, this preoccupation with origins, justifiable in a certain type of religious analysis, has spread in a doubtlessly inevitable contagion into other fields of research where its legitimacy is far more debatable. Moreover, history oriented towards origins was put to the service of value judgments. What else did Taine intend, in tracing the "origins" of the France of his day, but a denunciation of the political ill consequences of what he considered a false philosophy of man? And whether the subject was the Germanic invasions or the Norman conquest of England, the past was so assiduously used as an explanation of the present only in order that the present might be the better justified or condemned. So in many cases the demon of origins has been, perhaps, only the incarnation of that other satanic enemy of true history: the mania for making judgments.

But let us return to our Christian studies. It is one thing for a troubled and self-searching conscience to determine its attitude toward the Catholic religion by some such code as is daily laid down in our churches;

it is quite another for the historian to explain present-day Catholicism as an observed fact. A knowledge of their beginnings is indispensable to understand, but insufficient to account for, the actual religious phenomena. To simplify our problem, we must postpone the question as to how far the creed, identical in name, is the same in substance. Even assuming our religious tradition entirely unchanging, we must find reasons for its preservation. Human reasons, that is, for the assumption of divine intervention would be unscientific. In a word, the question is no longer whether Jesus was first crucified and then resurrected, but how it came to pass that so many fellow humans today believe in the Crucifixion and Resurrection. Now, wherever fidelity to a belief is to be found, all evidences agree that it is but one aspect of the general life of a group. It is like a knot in which are intertwined a host of divergent characteristics of the structure and mentality of a society. In short, a religious creed involves the whole problem of the human environment. Great oaks from little acorns grow. But only if they meet favorable conditions of soil and climate, conditions which are entirely beyond the scope of embryology.

Religious history has here been cited only by way of example. In any study, seeking the origins of a human activity, there lurks the same danger of confusing ancestry with explanation.

It is very like the illusion of certain old etymologists

who thought they had said all when they set down the oldest known meaning of a word opposite its present sense, having shown, for example, that *bureau* originally meant a coarse woolen cloth, or that *timbre* [4] meant a drum. As if the main problem were not to understand how and why the transition had taken place. As if, above all, the meaning of any word were influenced more by its own past than by the contemporary state of the vocabulary which, in its turn, is determined by the social conditions of the moment. *Bureaux* in *bureaux de ministère* means a bureaucracy. When I ask for *timbres* at my post-office window, I am able to use that term only because of recent technical changes, such as the organization of the postal service itself, and the substitution of a little gummed picture for the stamping of a postmark, which have revolutionized human communications. It is because the different acceptations of the old word, particularized according to profession, are today so widely different that there is no risk of confusion between the *timbre* which I glue on my envelope and the purity of *timbre* which the music salesman praises in his instruments.

We speak of the "origins of the feudal system." Where are we to seek them? Some say: "In Rome." Others: "In Germany." The cause of their confusion is obvious. Whether Roman or Germanic, certain practices, such as clientele relations, companionship in arms, and the use of land tenure as payment for serv-

[4] A postage stamp.

ice, were carried on by later generations in Europe during the ages we call "feudal." But such practices were modified a great deal. There were two words—"benefice" (*beneficium*) among the Latin, and "fief" among the German-speaking peoples—which these later generations persisted in using, while gradually and without realizing it, conferring upon them quite a new significance. For, to the great despair of historians, men fail to change their vocabulary every time they change their customs. All this is very interesting, but it does not tell us the causes of feudalism. The characteristic institutions of European feudalism were no mere patchwork of surviving scraps. At one stage in our history, they arose from a total social situation.

M. Seignobos has somewhere remarked: "I believe that the revolutionary thought of the eighteenth century . . . proceeds from the English thought of the seventeenth." Does he mean by this that the French publicists of the Enlightenment, having read or been indirectly influenced by certain English works of the preceding century, adopted their political principles from them? We might accept this thesis if we suppose that our *philosophes* contributed nothing original in the way of intellectual substance or atmospheric perspective to the foreign formulæ. But even arbitrarily reduced to a matter of borrowing, the history of this intellectual movement is far from being clear. For the problem is still to know why the transference of ideas took place when it did—no sooner and no later. A contagion supposes two things: microbe multiplication and, at the moment when the disease strikes, a favorable breeding-ground.

In a word, a historical phenomenon can never be understood apart from its moment in time. This is true of every evolutionary stage, our own and all others. As the old Arab proverb has it: "Men resemble their times more than they do their fathers." Disregard of this Oriental wisdom has sometimes brought discredit to the study of the past.

5. The Boundaries between Past and Present

Must we believe, because the past does not entirely account for the present, that it is utterly useless for its interpretation? The curious thing is that we should be able to ask the question today.

Not so very long ago, the answer was almost unanimously predetermined. "He who would confine his thought to present time will not understand present reality." So Michelet expressed it at the beginning of his *Peuple*—a fine book, but infected with the fever of the age in which it was written. And Leibniz before him ranked among those benefits which attend the study of history "the origins of things present which are to be found in things past; for a reality is never better understood than through its causes." [5]

But since Leibniz, and since Michelet, a great

[5] Preface to *Accessiones Historicæ* (1700), Opera, ed. Dutens, t. IV 2, p. 53: "*Tria sunt quæ expetimus in historia: primum, voluptatem noscendi res singulares; deinde, utilia in primis vitæ præcepta; ac denique origines præsentium a præteritus repetitas, cum omnia optime ex causis noscantur.*"

change has taken place. Successive technological revolutions have immeasurably widened the psychological gap between generations. With some reason, perhaps, the man of the age of electricity and of the airplane feels himself far removed from his ancestors. With less wisdom, he has been disposed to conclude that they have ceased to influence him. There is also a modernist twist inherent in the engineering mind. Is a mastery of old Volta's ideas about galvanism necessary to run or repair a dynamo? By what is unquestionably a lame analogy, but one which readily imposes itself upon more than one machine-dominated mentality, it is easy to think that an analysis of their antecedents is just as useless for the understanding and solving of the great human problems of the moment. Without fully recognizing it, the historians, too, are caught in this modernist climate. Why then should they not feel that, within their province, there has also been a shift in the line which separates the new from the old? What, for example, of the system of stabilized currency and the gold standard which, only yesterday, would have figured as the very norm of up-to-dateness in every manual of political economy? To the modern economist, do they belong to the present, or to a history already reeking with mold?

Behind these confused impressions, it is possible to discover a number of more consistent ideas, whose simplicity, at least on the surface, has captivated certain minds.

• • •

One short period seems somehow set apart from the vast sweep of time. Its beginning was relatively recent, and its end overlaps our own day. Nothing in it—neither its outstanding social and political characteristics, nor its physical equipment, nor its cultural tone—presents any important contrasts with our own world. It appears, in a word, to assume a very marked degree of "contemporaneousness" with us. And, from this, it derives the virtue or defect of being distinct from the rest of the past. A high-school teacher, who was very old when I was very young, once told us: "Since 1830, there has been no more history. It is all politics." One would no longer say "since 1830"—the July Days have grown old in their turn. Nor would one say: "It is all politics." Rather, with a respectful air: "It is all sociology." Or, with less respect: "It is all journalism." Nevertheless, there are many who would gladly repeat that since 1914, or since 1940, there has been no more history. Yet they would not agree very well in other respects as to the reasons for this ostracism.

Some, who consider that the most recent events are unsuitable for all really objective research just because they are recent, wish only to spare Clio's chastity from the profanation of present controversy. Such, I believe, was the thought of my old teacher. This is to rate our self-control rather low. It also quite overlooks that, once an emotional chord has been struck, the line between present and past is no longer strictly regulated by a mathematically measurable chronology. In the Languedoc high school where I served my first term as a teacher, my good headmaster issued a warning in a voice befitting a captain of education. "Here, with the nineteenth century, there is little danger; but when you touch on the religious wars, you must take great care! " In truth, whoever lacks the strength, while seated at his desk, to rid his mind of the virus of the present may readily permit its poison to infiltrate even a commentary on the *Iliad* or the *Ramayana*.

There are other savants who consider, quite to the contrary and with reason, that contemporary society is perfectly susceptible of scientific investigation. But they admit this only to reserve its study for branches of learning quite distinct from that which has the past for its object. They analyze, and they claim, for example, to understand the contemporary economic system on the basis of observations limited to a few decades. In a word, they consider the epoch in which we live as separated from its predecessors by contrasts so clear as to be self-explanatory. Such is also the instinctive attitude of a great many of the merely curious. The history of the remoter periods attracts them only as an innocuous intellectual luxury. On one hand, a small group of antiquarians taking a ghoulish delight in unwrapping the winding-sheets of the dead gods; on the other, sociologists, economists, and publicists, the only explorers of the living.

6. Understanding the Present by the Past

Under close scrutiny the prerogative of self-intelligibility thus attributed to present time is found to be based upon a set of strange postulates.

In the first place, it supposes that, within a generation or two, human affairs have undergone a change which is not merely rapid, but total, so that no institution of long standing, no traditional form of conduct, could have escaped the revolutions of the laboratory and the factory. It overlooks the force of inertia peculiar to so many social creations.

Man spends his time devising techniques of which he afterwards remains a more or less willing prisoner. What traveler in northern France has not been struck by the strange pattern of the fields? For centuries, changes in ownership have modified the original design; yet, even today, the sight of these inordinately long and narrow strips, dividing the arable land into a prodigious number of pieces, is something which baffles the scientific agriculturalist. The waste of effort which such a disposition entails and the problems which it imposes upon the cultivators are undeniable. How are we to account for it? Certain impatient publicists have replied: "By the Civil Code and its inevitable effects. Change the laws on inheritance and the evil will be removed." Had they known history better, or had they further questioned a peasant mentality shaped by centuries of experience, they would not have thought the cure so simple. Indeed, this pattern dates back to origins so distant that no scholar has yet succeeded in accounting for it satisfactorily. The settlers in the era of the dolmens have more to do with it than the lawyers of the First Empire. Perpetuating itself, as it were, of necessity, for want of correction, this ignorance of the past not only confuses contemporary science, but confounds contemporary action.

A society that could be completely molded by its immediately preceding period would have to have a structure so malleable as to be virtually invertebrate. It would also have to be a society in which communication between generations was conducted, so to speak, in "Indian file"—the children having contact with their ancestors only through the mediation of their parents.

Now, this is not true. It is not true even when the communication is purely oral. Take our villages, for example. Because working conditions keep the mother and father away almost all day, the young children are brought up chiefly by their grandparents. Consequently, with the molding of each new mind, there is a backward step, joining the most malleable to the most inflexible mentality, while skipping that generation which is the sponsor of change. There is small room for doubt that this is the source of that traditionalism inherent in so many peasant societies. The instance is particularly clear, but it is far from unique. Because the natural antagonism between age groups is always intensified between neighboring generations, more than one youth has learned at least as much from the aged as from those in their prime.

Still more strongly, between even widely scattered generations, the written word vastly facilitates those transfers of thought which supply the true continuity of a civilization. Take Luther, Calvin, Loyola, certainly men from another time—from the sixteenth century, in fact. The first duty of the historian who would understand and explain them will be to return them to their milieu, where they are immersed in the mental climate of their time and faced by problems of conscience rather different from our own. But who would dare to say that the understanding of the Protestant or the Catholic Reformation, several centuries removed, is not far more important for a proper grasp of the world today than a great many other movements of thought or feeling, which are certainly more recent, yet more ephemeral?

In a word, the fallacy is clear, and it is only necessary to formulate it in order to destroy it. It represents the course of human evolution as a series of short, violent jerks, no one of which exceeds the space of a few lifetimes. Observation proves, on the contrary, that the mighty convulsions of that vast, continuing development are perfectly capable of extending from the beginning of time to the present. What would we think of a geophysicist who, satisfied with having computed their remoteness to a fraction of an inch, would then conclude that the influence of the moon upon the earth is far greater than that of the sun? Neither in outer space, nor in time, can the potency of a force be measured by the single dimension of distance.

Finally, what of those things past which seem to have lost all authority over the present—faiths which have vanished without a trace, social forms which have miscarried, techniques which have perished? Would anyone think that, even among these, there is nothing useful for his understanding? That would be to forget that there is no true understanding without a certain range of comparison; provided, of course, that that comparison is based upon differing and, at the same time, related realities. One could scarcely deny that such is here the case.

Certainly, we no longer consider today, as Machiavelli wrote, and as Hume or Bonald thought, that there is, in time, "at least something which is changeless: that is man." We have learned that man, too, has changed a great deal in his mind and, no less certainly, in the most delicate organs of his body. How should it be otherwise? His mental climate has been greatly altered; and to no less an extent, so, too, have his hygiene and his diet. However, there must be a permanent foundation in human nature and in human society, or the very names of man or society become meaningless. How, then, are we to believe that we understand these men, if we study them only in their reactions to circumstances peculiar to a moment? It would be an inadequate test of them, even for that particular moment. A great many potentialities, which might at any instant emerge from concealment, a great many more or less unconscious drives behind individual or collective attitudes, would remain in the shadows. In a unique case the specific elements cannot be differentiated; hence an interpretation cannot be made.

7. Understanding the Past by the Present

This solidarity of the ages is so effective that the lines of connection work both ways. Misunderstanding of the present is the inevitable consequence of ignorance of the past. But a man may wear himself out just as fruitlessly in seeking to understand the past, if he is totally ignorant of the present. There is an anecdote which I have already recounted elsewhere: I had gone with Henri Pirenne to Stockholm; we had scarcely arrived, when he said to me: "What shall we go to see first? It seems that there is a new city hall here. Let's start there." Then, as if to ward off my surprise, he added: "If I were an antiquarian, I would have eyes only for old stuff, but I am a historian. Therefore, I love life." This faculty of understanding the living is, in very truth, the master quality of the historian. Despite their occasional frigidity of style, the greatest of our number have all possessed it. Fustel or Maitland, in their austere way, had it as much as Michelet. And, perhaps, it originates as a gift from the fairies, quite inaccessible to anyone who has not found it in his cradle. That does not lessen the obligation to exercise and develop it constantly. How? How better than by the example of Henri Pirenne—by keeping in constant touch with the present day?

For here, in the present, is immediately perceptible that vibrance of human life which only a great effort of the imagination can restore to the old texts. I have many times read, and I have often narrated, accounts of wars and battles. Did I truly know, in the full sense of that word, did I know from within, before I myself had suffered the terrible, sickening reality, what it meant for an army to be encircled, what it meant for a people to meet defeat? Before I myself had breathed the joy of victory in the summer and autumn of 1918 (and, although, alas! its perfume will not again be quite the same, I yearn to fill my lungs with it a second time) did I truly know all that was inherent in that beautiful word? In the last analysis, whether consciously or no, it is always by borrowing from our daily experiences and by shading them, where necessary, with new tints that we derive the elements which help us to restore the past. The very names we use to describe ancient ideas or vanished forms of social organization would be quite meaningless if we had not known living men. The value of these merely instinctive impressions will be increased a hundredfold if they are replaced by a ready and critical observation. A great mathematician would not, I suppose, be less great because blind to the world in which he lives. But the scholar who has no inclination to observe the men, the things, or the events around him will perhaps deserve the title, as Pirenne put it, of a useful antiquarian. He would be wise to renounce all claims to that of a historian.

Moreover, the cultivation of historical sensitivity is not always all that is involved. It may happen, in a given line, that the knowledge of the present bears even more immediately upon the understanding of the past.

It would be a grievous error, indeed, to think that the order which historians adopt for their inquiries must necessarily correspond to the sequence of events. Even though they restore its true direction afterwards, they have often benefited at the outset by reading history, as Maitland said, "backwards." For the natural progression of all research is from the best (or least badly) understood to the most obscure. Certainly, it is far from true that the light of documentation grows ever brighter as we pass down the corridor of the ages. For example, we are much less well-informed on the tenth century of our era than on the epoch of Cæsar or Augustus. In the majority of cases however, the nearest periods correspond better with the zones of relative clarity. We must add that, in proceeding mechanically from early to late, there is always the risk of wasting time in tracking down the beginning or causes of phenomena which, in the event, may turn out to be somewhat imaginary. The most illustrious among us have occasionally made strange mistakes through having neglected to pursue a prudently retrogressive method whenever and wherever it was indicated. Fustel de Coulanges devoted himself to the "origins" of feudal institutions of which he had formed, I fear, only a rather confused picture, and to the beginnings of a serfdom which, misled by secondhand descriptions, he conceived in entirely false colors.

Now, more often than is generally supposed, it happens that, in order to find daylight, the historian may have to pursue his subject right up to the present. In certain of its fundamental features, our rural landscape, as has been previously mentioned, dates from a very remote epoch. However, in order to interpret the rare documents which permit us to fathom its misty beginnings, in order to ask the right questions, even in order to know what we were talking about, it was necessary to fulfill a primary condition: that of observing and analyzing our present landscape. For it alone furnished those comprehensive vistas without which it was impossible to begin. Not, indeed, that there could be any question of imposing this forever-static picture, just as it is, at each stage of the journey upstream to the headwaters of the past. Here, as elsewhere, it is change which the historian is seeking to grasp. But in the film which he is examining, only the last picture remains quite clear. In order to reconstruct the faded features of the others, it behooves him first to unwind the spool in the opposite direction from that in which the pictures were taken.

. . .

There is, then, just one science of men in time. It requires us to join the study of the dead and of the living. What shall we call it? I have already explained why the ancient name, "history," seemed to me the best. It is the most comprehensive, the least exclusive, the most electric with stirring reminders of a more than age-old endeavor. In proposing to extend history right down to the present (contrary to certain prejudices which are not so old as history itself), I have no desire to expand the claims of my own profession. Life is too short, and science too vast, to permit even the greatest genius a total experience of humanity. Some men will always specialize in the present, as others do in the Stone Age or in Egyptology. We simply ask both to bear in mind that historical research will tolerate no autarchy. Isolated, each will understand only by halves, even within his own field of study; for the only true history, which can advance only through mutual aid, is universal history.

A science, however, is not to be defined entirely in terms of its object. Its limits can be fixed quite as well by the character of its appropriate methods.

It remains to be seen whether the techniques of inquiry should be considered fundamentally different according as the investigation approaches or recedes from the present. This, in its turn, suggests the entire problem of historical observation.

CHAPTER II

HISTORICAL OBSERVATION

1. General Characteristics of Historical Observation

To begin, let us place ourselves firmly in the study of the past.

The most obvious characteristics of historical information, in the ordinary and restricted sense of the term, have been frequently described. We are told that the historian is, by definition, absolutely incapable of observing the facts which he examines. No Egyptologist has ever seen Ramses. No expert on the Napoleonic Wars has ever heard the sound of the cannon at Austerlitz. We can speak of earlier ages only through the accounts of eye-witnesses. According to this view, we are in the predicament of a police magistrate who strives to reconstruct a crime he has not seen; of a physicist who, confined to his bed with grippe, hears the results of his experiments only through the reports of his laboratory technician. In short, in contrast to the knowledge of the present, that of the past is necessarily "indirect."

No one would dream of denying the element of truth in these remarks. Nevertheless, they demand considerable modification.

. . .

Let us suppose that a military commander has just won a victory. That, immediately, he sets to work writing an account in his own hand. That it was he who conceived the plan of the battle, and that it was he who directed it. And finally that, thanks to the moderate size of the field (for in order to sharpen the argument, we are imagining a battle of former times, drawn up in a confined space), he has been able to see almost the entire conflict develop before his eyes. Nevertheless, we cannot doubt that, in more than one essential episode, he will be forced to refer to the reports of his lieutenants. In acting thus as narrator, he would only be behaving as he had a few hours before in the action. Then as commander, regulating the movements of his troops to the swaying tide of battle, what sort of information shall we think to have served him best? Was it the rather confused scenes viewed through his binoculars, or the reports brought in hot haste by the couriers and aides-de-camp? Seldom can a leader of troops be his own observer. Meanwhile, even in so favorable a hypothesis as this, what has become of that marvel of "direct" observation which is claimed as the prerogative of the studies of the present?

In truth, it is scarcely ever anything but a delusion, at least as soon as the observer has expanded his horizon only slightly. A good half of all we see is seen through the eyes of others. As an economist, I follow trading developments for this month or for this week; I do so by means of statistics which I have not personally compiled. As a student of the present instant, I apply myself to the task of sounding public opinion on the important issues of the day. I ask questions. I note, compare, and compute the answers. What do I then have but the rather awkwardly expressed ideas which my communicants have formulated as to what they believe they believe, or what they are willing to reveal. These are the subjects of my experiments, but, whereas the physiologist who dissects a guinea pig sees with his own eyes the lesion or abnormality which has been the object of his search, I know the mood of my "man in the street" only through the chart of it which he himself agrees to draw for me. Because the individual, narrowly restricted by his senses and power of concentration, never perceives more than a tiny patch of the vast tapestry of events, deeds, and words which form the destinies of a group, and because, moreover, he possesses an immediate awareness of only his own mental state, all knowledge of mankind, to whatever time it applies, will always derive a large part of its evidence from others. In this respect, the student of the present is scarcely any better off than the historian of the past.

But there is more. Is it certain that the observation of the past, even of the very remote past, is always "indirect"?

It is easy to see why this remoteness of the scholar from the object of his knowledge makes so strong an impression upon many historical theorists. It is because they think of history primarily in terms of events, even of episodes—of a history which, rightly or wrongly (and it is immaterial at the moment) attaches an extreme importance to the exact reconstruction of the actions, words, or attitudes of a few personages, brought together for a relatively brief scene, in which, as in a classic tragedy, are marshaled all the forces of the critical moment: the day of a revolution, a battle, or a diplomatic interview. It is related that on September 2, 1792, the head of the Princess de Lamballe was paraded on the end of a pike under the windows of the royal family. Is this true or false? M. Pierre Caron, who has written an admirably honest book on the September Massacres, does not venture an opinion. Had he been permitted to watch the ghastly cortege in person from a tower in the Temple, he would have known what to think—at least if, preserving his scholarly detachment in these circumstances (as might be expected), and properly mistrustful of his own memory, he had further taken the precaution of making a note of his observations on the spot. Unquestionably, in such cases, the historian is mortified by comparing his position with that of a reliable witness of a present event. He is as if at the rear of a column, in which the news travels from the head back through the ranks. It is not a good vantage-point from which to gather correct information. Not so very long ago, during a relief march at night, I saw the word passed down the length of a column in this manner: "Look out! Shell holes to the left!" The last man received it in the form, "To the left!" took a step in that direction, and fell in.

There are other contingencies, however. Archæologists have restored to the light of the present day a number of pottery urns, filled with the bones of children, which had been securely sealed up in the walls of certain Syrian fortresses built several thousand years before the birth of Christ. Since we cannot reasonably suppose that these bones have strayed there by accident, according to all the evidence, we are confronted with the remains of human sacrifices, performed at the moment of original construction and somehow connected with it. As to the beliefs which were expressed in these rites, we must refer to contemporary testimony, or, if none exists, proceed by analogy with the aid of other evidence. For how are we to understand a faith we do not share except through the accounts of others? Such—and it bears repeating—is the case with all phenomena of consciousness in so far as they are alien to us. As for the mere fact of sacrifice, on the other hand, our situation is very different. To be sure, we no more grasp the fact immediately, properly speaking, than the geologist captures the living ammonite when he discovers its fossil, or than a physicist sees the actual molecular motion when he studies its effects in a suspension, as in Brownian movement. But the simple reasoning which, by eliminating all other possible explanations, permits us to pass from the authenticated object to the fact of which it is the proof, this act of rudimentary interpretation—bordering, indeed, upon those instinctive mental reactions without which no sensation would become a perception—in no way requires the intervention of another observer between the object and ourselves. By "indirect knowledge" the methodologists have generally understood that which arrives at the mind of the historian only by way of other human minds. The phrase is not, perhaps, very carefully chosen; it confines itself to pointing out the presence of an intermediary, without making it clear why this intermediary should necessarily be human. But let us accept the common usage without further quibbling. In that sense, there is certainly nothing indirect about our knowledge of these immured sacrifices in ancient Syria.

Now, a great many other vestiges of the past are equally accessible. Such is the case not only with almost all the vast bulk of the unwritten evidence, but also with a good part of that which is written. If the best-known theorists of our methods had not shown such an astonishing and arrogant indifference toward the techniques of archæology, if they had not been as obsessed with narrative in the category of documents as they were with incident in the category of actions, they would doubtless have been less ready to throw us back upon an eternally dependent method of observation. In the royal tombs of Ur in Chaldea, there have been found beads of necklaces made of amazonite. As the nearest deposits of this mineral are located either in the heart of India or in the neighborhood of Lake Baikal, it has seemed obvious to conclude that, as far back as the third millennium before Christ, the cities of the lower Euphrates maintained trading relations with some very distant lands. The inference may be either true or false. However that may be, it is undeniable that it is an induction of the most classic type; it is founded upon the observation of a fact and the word of another person has absolutely nothing to do with it. But physical objects are far from being the only ones which can be thus readily apprehended at firsthand. A linguistic characteristic, a point of law embodied in a text, a rite, as defined by a book of ceremonial or represented on a stele, are realities just as much as the flint, hewn of yore by the artisan of the stone age—realities which we ourselves apprehend and elaborate by a strictly personal effort of the intelligence. There is no need to appeal to any other human mind as an interpreter. To revert to our analogy of a moment ago, it is not true that the historian can see what goes on in his laboratory only through the eyes of another person. To be sure, he never arrives until after the experiment has been concluded. But, under favorable circumstances, the experiment leaves behind certain residues which he can see with his own eyes.

It is therefore advisable to define the indisputable peculiarities of historical observation in terms which are both less ambiguous and more comprehensive.

Its primary characteristic is the fact that knowledge of all human activities in the past, as well as of the greater part of those in the present, is, as François Simiand aptly phrased it, a knowledge of their tracks. Whether it is the bones immured in the Syrian fortifications, a word whose form or use reveals a custom, a narrative written by the witness of some scene, ancient or modern, what do we really mean by *document*, if it is not a "track," as it were—the mark, perceptible to the senses, which some phenomenon, in itself inaccessible, has left behind?

It matters little whether the original object is by its very nature inaccessible to the senses, like an atom whose trajectory is rendered visible in a Crookes tube, or whether through the effect of time it has only become so in the present, like the fern, rotting for thousands of years, whose imprint is left upon a lump of coal, or like those long-abandoned ceremonials which are painted and explained upon the walls of Egyptian temples. In either case, the process of reconstruction is the same, and every science offers a variety of examples of it.

However, the fact that many explorers in every field are able to understand certain central phenomena only by means of other phenomena derived from them in this manner by no means signifies that they all share a perfect equality of methods. Like the physicists, they may themselves be able to produce the appearance of these "tracks." On the other hand, they may be compelled to wait upon the caprice of forces over which they have no influence whatsoever. Depending on these alternatives, their positions will vary widely. What is the situation of the observers of human activity? Here the question of chronology again arises.

The fact that all moderately complex human acts elude the possibility either of reproduction or of deliberate initiation seems to go without saying, and, in any case, we shall return to the point later. To be sure, there are psychological tests to measure the most elementary sensations as well as the most delicate nuances of intelligence or emotivity. But these are applicable only to the individual. They are almost entirely unsuited to group psychology. One can not—even if one could, one would dare not—deliberately produce a panic or a movement of religious fervor. However, if the phenomena under study belong to the present or to the very recent past, the observer—however impotent he may be to force their repetition or to shape their development to his liking—is not equally helpless as regards their "tracks." Certain of these he is able literally to call into existence. These are the reports of witnesses.

It was as impossible to relive the experience of Austerlitz on December 5, 1805, as it is today. However, suppose that the question was what such and such a regiment had done in the battle? Had Napoleon wished to inform himself on this point, several hours after the cease-fire, he had but to say the word to have an officer give him an account. If no such report, public or private, was ever made, or if those which were written were lost, then it would be vain for us to ask Napoleon's question; it stands a good chance of never being answered, along with many others far more important. What historian has not had day-dreams of being able, like Ulysses, to body forth the shades for questioning? But it is no longer the season of the miracles of the Nekuia, and we have no other device for returning through time except that which operates in our minds with the materials provided by past generations.

The advantages of the present must not be exaggerated. Let us imagine that all the officers and men of the hypothetical regiment at Austerlitz have perished, or, more simply, that among the survivors there are no longer to be found witnesses whose memory and powers of attention are trustworthy. Napoleon would then be no better off than we are. Anyone who has taken even the humblest part in a great battle is very well aware that it sometimes becomes impossible to be precise about a major episode after only a few hours. We must add that not all "tracks" lend themselves equally well to this evocation of the past for the edification of the future. If the customs had neglected to register the imports and exports of merchandise every day in November 1942, I would have in December practically no means of determining the foreign commerce of a month before. In a word, the difference between the study of the remote and that of the recent past is, as previously stated, only one of degree. It does not extend to the fundamental problem of method. Still, the difference is important, and it is only proper to examine the consequences.

The past is, by definition, a datum which nothing in the future will change. But the knowledge of the past is something progressive which is constantly transforming and perfecting itself. Anyone who doubts this need only recall how much it has improved under our very eyes in little more than a century. Vast areas of mankind have emerged from the shadows. Egypt and Chaldea have shaken off their shrouds. The lost cities of central Asia have disclosed their now-unspoken languages and long-extinct religions. A civilization, all unsuspected, has but lately risen from its grave upon the banks of the Indus. That is not all, and the ingenuity of the scholars in further ransacking the libraries or in opening new excavations on ancient sites is neither the sole nor, perhaps, even the most effective means of enriching our picture of the past. Hitherto-unknown techniques of investigation have also come to light. We are more skillful than our predecessors in examining languages for the evidence of customs and tools for the evidence of techniques. Above all, we have learned how to probe more deeply in the analysis of social developments. The study of popular rites and beliefs is barely sketching its first outlines. Economic history, which, not so long ago, Cournot did not even think to include in his listing of the various aspects of historical research, is only beginning to establish itself.

All this is certain. All of it offers us the most extensive hopes, but they are not unlimited hopes. This sense of virtually unlimited progress, granted to a science like chemistry, which is capable of creating even its own subject matter, is refused to us. Explorers of the past are never quite free. The past is their tyrant. It forbids them to know anything which it has not itself, consciously or otherwise, yielded to them. We shall never establish a statistical table of prices for the Merovingian epoch, for there are no documents which record these prices in sufficient number. We shall never be able to get inside the minds of the men of eleventh-century Europe, for example, as well as we can those of the contemporaries of Pascal or Voltaire, because, in place of their private letters or confessions, we have only a few bad biographies, written in a conventional style. Owing to this gap, one entire segment of our history necessarily assumes the rather anemic aspect of a world without individuals. But we must not grumble too much. We poor adepts of the young sciences of man are often laughed at, but, in our strict submission to an inflexible fate, we are no worse off than many of our confreres in the older and safer disciplines. Such is the common lot of all studies calling for the examination of past phenomena. The prehistorian who lacks written records is no more incapable of reconstructing the rituals of the stone age than is the paleontologist (I suppose) of reconstructing the glands of internal secretion of the plesiosaurus whose skeleton alone still remains. It is always disagreeable to say: "I do not know. I cannot know." It must not be said except after an energetic, even a desperate search. But there are times when the sternest duty of the savant, who has first tried every means, is to resign himself to his ignorance and to admit it honestly.

2. *Evidence*

"Herodotus of Thurii here sets down his inquiries toward the end that the things done by men should not be forgotten with the passage of time and that the great and marvelous exploits, performed by both Greeks and barbarians, should not lose their radiance." Thus begins what, with the exception of a few fragments, is the oldest book of history which has come down to us in the Western world. For the sake of illustration, let us compare it with one of the guides for the trip to the beyond which the Egyptians put into their tombs in the time of the Pharaohs. We shall then have face to face the archetypes of the two chief categories into which the innumerable varieties of documents at the disposal of the historian are divided. The evidence of the first group is intentional; that of the second is not.

Indeed, when in seeking information we read Herodotus, Froissart, the memoirs of Marshal Joffre, or the completely contradictory accounts, reported these days in the British or German newspapers, of an attack on a Mediterranean convoy, we are only doing exactly what the writers expected us to do. On the other hand, the formulæ of the Book of the Dead were destined only to be recited by the soul in peril and heard by gods alone. The lake-dweller who threw his garbage into the near-by water, where the archæologists retrieve it today, wanted only to keep his hut clean. The bull of papal immunity was so carefully preserved in the strongbox of the monastery only in order, when the time arrived, that it might be brandished under the nose of a meddling bishop. In none of these precautions was there the least desire to influence the opinions either of contemporaries or of future historians; and when the medievalist, in this year of our Lord 1942, leafs through the archives of the commercial correspondence of the Cedame family of Lucca, he is guilty of an indiscretion which would be loudly decried by the financiers of our own day, if he took the same liberty with their files.

Now, the narrative sources—to use a rather baroque but hallowed phrase—that is, the accounts which are consciously intended to inform their readers, still continue to provide valuable assistance to the scholar. Among their other advantages, they are ordinarily the only ones which furnish a chronological framework, however inconsistent. What would not the prehistorian or the historian of India give to have a Herodotus at his disposal? Nevertheless, there can be no doubt that, in the course of its development, historical research has gradually been led to place more and more confidence in the second category of evidence, in the evidence of witnesses in spite of themselves. We have only to compare the Roman history of Rollin or even that of Niebuhr with any of those short summaries we read today. The former draw the heart of their matter from Livy, Suetonius, or Florus. The latter are constructed in large measure out of inscriptions, papyri, and coins. Only in this way could whole sections of the past have been reconstructed. This is true of all prehistory, as well as of almost all economic history and almost all history of social structures. Even in the present, who among us would not prefer to get hold of a few secret chancellery papers or some confidential military reports, to having all the newspapers of 1938 or 1939?

It is not that this sort of document is any less subject to errors or falsehoods than the others. There are plenty of fraudulent bulls, and neither all ambassadorial accounts nor all business letters tell the truth. But this kind of distortion, if it exists, at least, has not been especially designed to deceive posterity. Moreover, these tracks which the past unwittingly leaves all along its trail do more than simply permit us to fill in the narrative where it is missing and to check it where its truthfulness is suspected. They protect our studies from a peril more deadly then either ignorance or inaccuracy: that of an incurable sclerosis. Indeed, without their aid, every time the historian turned his attention to the generations gone by, he would become the inevitable prey of the same prejudices, false inhibitions, and myopias which had plagued the vision of those same generations. For example, the medievalists would accord but a trivial significance to communal development, under the pretext that the writers of the Middle Ages did not discuss it freely with their public, or would disregard the mighty force of religious life for the good reason that it occupied a much less important place in contemporary narrative literature than the wars of the barons. In a word, to resort to a favorite figure of Michelet's, history would become less the ever-daring explorer of the ages past than the eternally unmoving pupil of their "chronicles."

Moreover, even when most anxious to bear witness, that which the text tells us expressly has ceased to be the primary object of our attention today. Ordinarily, we prick up our ears far more eagerly when we are permitted to overhear what was never intended to be said. What do we find most instructive in the works of Saint-Simon? Is it their frequently fictitious news of the events of the reign, or the remarkable light which the *Memoirs* throw upon the mentality of a great noble at the court of the Sun King? At least three fourths of the lives of the saints of the high Middle Ages can teach us nothing concrete about those pious personages whose careers they pretend to describe. If, on the other hand, we consult them as to the way of life or thought peculiar to the epoch in which they were written (all things which the biographer of the saint had not the least intention of revealing), we shall find them invaluable. Despite our inevitable subordination to the past, we have freed ourselves at least to the extent that, eternally condemned to know only by means of its "tracks," we are nevertheless successful in knowing far more of the past than the past itself had thought good to tell us. Properly speaking, it is a glorious victory of mind over its material.

But from the moment when we are no longer resigned to purely and simply recording the words of our witnesses, from the moment we decide to force them to speak, even against their will, cross-examination becomes more necessary than ever. Indeed, it is the prime necessity of well-conducted historical research.

Many people and, it appears, even some authors of manuals entertain an extraordinarily simplified notion of our working procedure. First, as they are only too eager to tell you, there are the documents. The historian collects them, reads them, attempts to weigh their authenticity and truthfulness. Then, and only then, he makes use of them. There is only one trouble with this idea: no historian has ever worked in such a way, even when, by some caprice, he fancied that he was doing so.

For even those texts or archæological documents which seem the clearest and the most accommodating will speak only when they are properly questioned. Before Boucher de Perthes, as in our own day, there was plenty of flint artifacts in the alluvium of the Somme. However, there was no one to ask questions, and there was therefore no prehistory. As an old medievalist, I know nothing which is better reading than a cartulary. That is because I know just about what to ask it. A collection of Roman inscriptions, on the other hand, would tell me little. I know more or less how to read them, but not how to cross-question them. In other words, every historical research supposes that the inquiry has a direction at the very first step. In the beginning, there must be the guiding spirit. Mere passive observation, even supposing such a thing were possible, has never contributed anything productive to any science.

Indeed, we must here make no mistake. It may well be that the cross-examination remains purely instinctive. It is there, nevertheless. Without the scholar's being aware of it, its dictates are etched into his brain by the convictions and inhibitions of his former experiences, by means of tradition and by means of common sense, which is too often to say by means of vulgar prejudices. We are never quite so receptive as we should like to believe. There is no worse advice for a beginner than that he should simply sit patiently waiting for the inspiration of a document. Such conduct has betrayed more than one well-intended inquiry into either stalemate or checkmate.

Naturally, the method of cross-examination must be very elastic, so that it may change its direction or improvise freely for any contingency, yet be able, from the outset, to act as a magnet drawing findings out of the document. Even when he has settled his itinerary, the explorer is well aware that he will not follow it exactly. Without it, however, he would risk wandering perpetually at random.

The variety of historical evidence is nearly infinite. Everything that man says or writes, everything that he makes, everything he touches can and ought to teach us about him. It is curious to note how many people, unacquainted with our work, underestimate the true extent of its possibilities. It is because they persist in an idea of our science which dates back to the time when we scarcely knew how to read even the intentional evidence. In reproaching "traditional history," Paul Valéry has cited "the conquest of the earth" by electricity, as an example of one of those "notable phenomena" which it neglects, despite the fact that they have "more meaning and greater possibilities of shaping our immediate future than all the political events combined." For this, he deserves our heartiest applause. It is unfortunate, but all too true that this vast subject has still received no serious treatment. However, apparently led astray by an excess of severity to excuse the very fault which he has just condemned, Valéry adds that this phenomenon must of necessity elude the historian because, he argues, there are no documents which refer to it specifically. This time, shifting from the scholar to the science, he lodges his complaint at the wrong door. Who believes that the electrical companies have no archives, no records of consumption, no charts of the enlargement of their networks? The truth is that the historians until now have simply neglected to question these documents. Certainly, they are very much to blame, unless the fault lies with the custodians of the archives, possibly too jealous of their precious treasures. Have patience. History is not yet what it ought to be. That is no reason to make history as it can be the scapegoat for the sins which belong to bad history alone.

Marvelous as is the diversity of our materials, it nevertheless creates a difficulty so serious as to rank among the three or four outstanding paradoxes of the historical profession.

It would be sheer fantasy to imagine that for each historical problem there is a unique type of document with a specific sort of use. On the contrary, the deeper the research, the more the light of the evidence must converge from sources of many different kinds. What religious historian would be satisfied by examining a few theological tracts or hymnals? He knows full well that the painting and sculpture of sanctuary walls and the arrangement and furnishings of tombs have at least as much to tell him about dead beliefs and feelings as a thousand contemporary manuscripts. Our knowledge of the Germanic invasions has derived as much from the archæology of tombs and place-names as it has from the examination of charters and chronicles. As we approach our own times, the requirements change without becoming less exacting. To understand modern society, is it enough merely to plunge into reading parliamentary debates or cabinet papers? Is it not also necessary to be able to interpret a financial statement, as unintelligible to the layman as so many hieroglyphics? In an age when the machine is supreme, should a historian be allowed to ignore how machines are designed and modified?

Now, if almost any important human problem thus demands the handling of diverse types of evidence, on the other hand the types of evidence necessarily mark off the several branches of technical scholarship. The apprenticeship of each is long, but full mastery demands a still longer and almost constant practice. For example, very few scholars can boast that they are equally well equipped to read critically a medieval charter, to explain correctly the etymology of place-names, to date unerringly the ruins of dwellings of the prehistoric, Celtic, or Gallo-Roman periods, and to analyze the plant life proper to a pasture, a field, or a moor. Without all these, however, how could one pretend to describe the history of land use? Few sciences, I believe, are forced to use so many dissimilar tools at the same time. However, man's actions are the most complex in the animal kingdom, because man stands upon nature's summit.

It is advisable and, in my opinion, it is indispensable that the historian possess at least a smattering of all the principal techniques of his trade, if only to learn the strength of his tools and the difficulties of handling them. The list of "auxiliary disciplines" which we expect our beginners to learn is much too short. What an absurd illogicality that men who half the time can have access to their subject only through words, are permitted, among other deficiencies, to be ignorant of the fundamental attainments of linguistics!

But whatever the variety of accomplishments we may wish to ascribe to our best-equipped scholars, they will inevitably and, ordinarily very quickly, discover their own limitations. We have no other remedy than to substitute, in place of the multiple skills of a single man, the pooling of the techniques, practiced by different scholars, but all tending to throw light upon a specific subject. This method presupposes a spirit of teamwork. It also demands the preliminary definition by common consent of the several dominant problems. We are still all too distant from these goals. Nevertheless, in large measure, they will unquestionably govern the future of our science.

3 The Transmission of Evidence

One of the most difficult tasks of the historian is that of assembling those documents which he considers necessary. He could hardly succeed without the help of various guides: archival or library catalogues, museum indexes, and bibliographies of every kind. There are people who express contemptuous amazement at the time sacrificed by some scholars in composing such works and by all the rest in familiarizing themselves with their existence and use. They behave as if the most frightful waste of energy were not ultimately avoided, thanks to the hours thus devoted to labors which, if not without a certain hidden charm, are certainly lacking in romantic glamor. Let us suppose that I have become duly interested in the history of the cult of the saints, but that I am ignorant of the *Bibliotheca Hagiographica Latina* of the Bollandist Fathers. It would be difficult for anyone who is not an expert to imagine the amount of stupidly useless effort which this gap in my mental equipment would inevitably cost me. What is truly regrettable is not that we must stock our libraries with a considerable quantity of those tools, whose very enumeration, subject by subject, belongs to special books of orientation. It is rather that there are still not enough of them, especially for the most recent periods; that their composition, particularly in France, has conformed only by exception to a rational and comprehensive plan; and, finally, that the task of keeping them up to date has been too often abandoned either to the caprice of individuals or to the ill-advised parsimony of a few publishing houses. The first volume of Émile Molinier's admirable *Sources de l'Histoire de France* has not been revised since its first appearance in 1901. That simple fact is in itself a severe indictment. Granted that instruments do not create science, nevertheless a society which pretends to respect the sciences ought not to neglect their instruments. Nor would it be wise to rely entirely upon academic bodies for these instruments, for their methods of recruiting, favoring seniority and orthodox scholarship, do not particularly incline them to a spirit of enterprise. Our War College and General Staff are not the only institutions in France which have preserved the mentality of the oxcart in the age of the automobile.

Such guides, however well made, however abundant, would be of little aid to the worker who had no preliminary idea of the terrain to be explored. Despite what the beginners sometimes seem to imagine, documents do not suddenly materialize, in one place or another, as if by some mysterious decree of the gods. Their presence or absence in the depths of this archive or that library are due to human causes which by no means elude analysis. The problems posed by their transmission, far from having importance only for the technical experts, are most intimately connected with the life of the past, for what is here at stake is nothing less than the passing down of memory from one generation to another. In historical works of a serious nature, the author generally lists the files of archives he has examined and the printed collections he has used. That is all very well, but it is not enough. Every historical book worthy of the name ought to include a chapter, or if one prefers, a series of paragraphs inserted at turning points in the development, which might almost be entitled: "How can I know what I am about to say?" I am persuaded that even the lay reader would experience an actual intellectual pleasure in examining these "confessions." The sight of an investigation, with its successes and reverses, is seldom boring. It is the ready-made article which is cold and dull.

. . .

Sometimes I receive visits from people who wish to write the history of their village. Regularly, I give them the following standard advice, which I shall here simplify only a little in order to avoid the irrelevant scholarly details. "Except in recent times, peasant communities have rarely had any archives. The seigneuries on the other hand, as relatively well-organized and lasting enterprises, usually kept their papers from early times. For all the period prior to 1789, therefore, and especially for the most ancient times, the principal documents which you can hope to use will be of seigneurial origin. The result is that the first question you will have to answer, and upon which almost everything hinges, is this: Who was the seigneur of the town in 1789?" (Actually, it is not at all improbable that there were several seigneurs at the same time, sharing the village between them, but we shall discard this supposition in the interest of brevity.) "Three eventualities are conceivable. The seigneury could have belonged to a church, to a layman who emigrated during the Revolution, or, to a layman who did not emigrate. The first instance is by all odds the most favorable. The chances are that the records are both older and better kept. They were certainly confiscated in 1790, along with the land, under the Civil Constitution of the Clergy. Since they were then carried to some public place, we have reason to hope that they are still there today, more or less intact, and at the disposal of scholars. The hypothesis of the emigré is also promising. In this instance, too, the records should have been seized and transferred, although the outside chance of their willful destruction, as a vestige of a hatred regime, is rather more to be feared. The last possibility remains. It might prove infinitely troublesome. The former nobles, if they did not leave France, or in some other way fall afoul the laws of public safety, were not at all disturbed in their property. Of course, they lost their seigneurial rights, because these had been universally abolished, but they kept all their personal property and, consequently, their business papers. Since they were never confiscated by the state, the papers we are seeking, in this third case, met the common fate of all family papers. Even if they have not been lost, eaten by rats, or scattered by the caprice of sale or inheritance through the attics of three or four houses on different estates, there is nothing to oblige their present owners to let you see them."

I have cited this example, because it seems to me entirely typical of the conditions which frequently determine and limit documentation. A closer analysis will not be without interest.

We have just witnessed the revolutionary confiscations playing the role of a deity who often favors the scholar: the goddess Catastrophe. Innumerable Roman *municipia* have been transformed into banal little Italian villages, from which the archæologist unearths some few vestiges of antiquity with difficulty. Only the eruption of Vesuvius preserved Pompeii.

Certainly, the great disasters have not consistently

served history. The invaluable papers of the imperial Roman bureaucracy, as well as heaps of literary and historiographical manuscripts, were engulfed in the disorder of the Invasion. Before our very eyes, two world wars have razed monuments and storehouses of archives from a soil steeped in a glorious tradition. Nevermore shall we be able to leaf through the letters of the merchants of ancient Ypres. During the rout, I saw the order book of an army intentionally burnt.

Nevertheless, the peaceable continuity of social existence is much less favorable to the transmission of memory than is sometimes supposed. Revolutions force the doors of safes, and put ministers to flight before they have had time to burn their secret papers. In early judicial archives, the bankruptcy records yield up to us the papers of business concerns which, had they been permitted to live out a profitable and honorable existence, would inevitably have turned over the contents of their files to the pulp machines. Thanks to the admirable permanence of monastic institutions, the abbey of St. Denis still preserved in 1789 the charters which had been granted to it by the Merovingian kings a thousand years before. Yet it is in the National Archives that we read them today. Had the monks of St. Denis survived the revolution, is it certain that they would permit us to rummage through their coffers? Not very certain, I fear, since the Company of Jesus does not permit the profane an access to its collections, without which so many problems of modern history will always remain hopelessly obscure, and the

Bank of France does not invite experts on the First Empire to examine even its dustiest records. Indeed, the spirit of the secret society is inherent in all corporations. Here it is that the historian of the present finds himself plainly at a disadvantage: he is almost totally deprived of these unintentional confidences. For compensation, it is true, he has at his disposal the indiscretions which his friends whisper in his ear. Their intelligence, alas, is difficult to distingush from gossip. A good cataclysm suits our business better.

So it will be, at least, until society begins to organize a rational self-knowledge by controlling its records, instead of depending on calamities for its information. To do so, it must come to grips with the two principles responsible for forgetfulness and ignorance: that negligence which loses documents; and, even more dangerous, that passion for secrecy—diplomatic secrecy, business secrecy, family secrecy—which hides or destroys them. It is natural that the notary should be forbidden to reveal his client's transactions. But the laws which permit him to shroud the contracts of his great-grandfather's clients in the same impenetrable mystery—whereas, nothing strictly hinders his letting their papers turn to dust—are truly antediluvian. The motives which prompt the majority of great corporations to refuse to make public statistics absolutely indispensable for the sound conduct of the national economy are seldom respectable. Our civilization will take an immense forward stride on the day when concealment, raised to a rule of action and almost to a bourgeois virtue, shall give way to the desire for information, which is necessarily the desire to exchange information.

But let us get back to our village. The circumstances which, in this particular instance, have determined the loss or the preservation, the accessibility or the inaccessibility of the evidences have their origins in historical forces of a general nature. They present no feature which is not perfectly intelligible, but they are stripped of all logical connection with the object of the inquiry even though the result of that inquiry is found to depend upon them. For it is not immediately clear why, for example, the study of a little rural community in the Middle Ages should be more or less informative, according as its owner, several centuries later, should or should not have taken it into his head to join the forces assembling at Coblenz. Nothing is more prevalent than this paradox. If we know infinitely more about Roman Egypt than about Gaul in the same period, it is not because we are more interested in the Egyptians than in the Gallo-Romans: rather, it is that the dryness, the sand, and the rites of mummification have there preserved writings which the climate and customs of the Occident condemned to rapid destruction. The causes which make for success or failure in the search for documents ordinarily have nothing in common with the reasons which render these documents desirable: this inevitable element of the irrational imparts to our research a tinge of that inner tragedy in which, perhaps, so many creations of the mind discover not only their limitations but one of the secret reasons for their failure.

Again, in the example cited above, the fate of the documents, village by village, once the decisive facts were known, became almost predictable. Such is not always the case. Sometimes the result depends on the final intertwining of so many independent lines of causation that all prediction proves impossible. I know that four successive conflagrations, and then a plundering, devastated the archives of the ancient abbey of Saint Benoît-sur-Loire. How, on this basis, could I guess in advance what sort of papers these ravages have chosen to spare? What has been called the migration of manuscripts is, in itself, an extremely interesting subject of study. The progress of a literary work through the libraries, the execution of copies, and the care or negligence of librarians and copyists fully correspond to the vicissitudes and interplay of the cultural main streams of real life. But could even the best-informed scholar have predicted, prior to the discovery, that the sole manuscript of Tacitus' *Germania* would come up high and dry in the sixteenth century in the monastery of Herzfeld? In a word, at the bottom of nearly every search for documents there is a residue of the unexpected and, hence, of the fortuitous. A fellow worker, whom I knew well, once told me this story: On a shell-torn beach at Dunkerque, he was awaiting a doubtful rescue without betraying too much impatience when one of his comrades addressed him with a look of amazement. "Extraordinary! You don't even seem to mind this awful uncertainty!" My friend could have answered that, despite the popular prejudice, the mental climate of research is not so unsympathetic to ready acceptance of the lottery of fate.

A while ago we asked whether there is an antithesis of technique between knowledge of the past and of the present. The answer has already been given. Certainly, the explorers of the present and those of remoter times have each their particular way of handling their tools. Moreover, both have their advantages, depending on the particular case. The former have a more tangible grasp of life; but the latter in their investigations command means which are often denied to the first. Thus, the dissection of a cadaver discloses to the biologist many secrets which the study of a living subject would fail to reveal, but is mute about many others which are evident only in the living body. But, to whatever age of mankind the scholar turns, the methods of observation remain almost uniformly dependent upon "tracks," and are, therefore, fundamentally the same. So, too, as we shall see, are those critical rules which observation must obey if it is to be fruitful.

CHAPTER III

HISTORICAL CRITICISM

1. An Outline of the History of the Critical Method

THE MOST naïve policeman knows that a witness should not always be taken at his word, even if he does not always take full advantage of this theoretical knowledge. Similarly, it has been many a day since men first took it into their heads not to accept all historical evidence blindly. An experience almost as old as mankind has taught us that more than one manuscript has falsified its date or origin, that all the accounts are not true, and that even the physical evidences can be faked. In the Middle Ages, in the face of an abundance of forgeries, doubt was frequently a natural defensive reflex. "With ink, anyone can write anything." Thus exclaimed an eleventh-century country squire of Lorraine in reference to some monks who had armed themselves in a lawsuit against him with documentary proofs. The Donation of Constantine—that extraordinary literary concoction which a Roman cleric of the eighth century ascribed to the first Christian emperor—was contested, three centuries later, in the circle of the eminently pious Otto III. False relics have been hunted down almost from the first.

However, skepticism on principle is neither a more

estimable nor a more productive intellectual attitude than the credulity with which it is frequently blended in the simpler minds. In the first war, I knew a worthy veterinarian who, with some justification, refused categorically to believe anything in the newspapers. Yet the fellow swallowed hook, line, and sinker the most nonsensical hocus-pocus which any chance companion might pour in his eager ear.

Similarly, the criticism of ordinary common sense, for long the only one in use, and still somehow seductive to certain minds, cannot lead very far. In reality, this pretended common sense usually turns out to be nothing more than a compound of irrational postulates and hastily generalized experiences. As regards the physical world, it has denied the existence of the antipodes. It still denies the Einsteinian universe. It treated as mere legend Herodotus' tale reporting that, when turning the coast of Africa, the navigators saw the point from which the sun rises pass from their left to their right. As it regards human actions, on the other hand, the worst of common sense is that it exalts to the level of the eternal observations necessarily borrowed from our own brief moment of time. This is the principal vice of the Voltairian criticism, which is so penetrating in other respects. Above and beyond the peculiarities of individuals of every age, there are states of mind which were formerly common, yet which appear peculiar to us because we no longer share them. "Common sense," it seems, would refuse to accept the idea that Emperor Otto I could have signed, in favor of the Pope, grants of territories which could never be made good, since they both belied his former actions and were ignored in those that followed. Since his grant was incontestably authentic, however, we are forced to believe that his mentality was different from ours and, more particularly, that there was in his time a gap between words and deeds which surprises us today.

True progress began on the day when, as Volney put it, doubt became an "examiner"; or, in other words, when there had gradually been worked out objective rules which permitted the separation of truth from falsehood. The Jesuit Papebroeck, in whom the reading of *The Lives of the Saints* had instilled a profound mistrust of the entire heritage of the early Middle Ages, considered all the Merovingian charters which had been preserved in the monasteries as forgeries. No, replied Mabillon. There are unquestionably some charters which have been retouched, some which have been interpolated, and some which have been forged in their entirety. There are also some which are authentic, and this is how it is possible to distinguish the bad from the good. That year, 1681, the year of the publication of the *De Re Diplomatica*, was truly a great one in the history of the human mind, for the criticism of the documents of archives was definitely established.

Moreover, it was in every respect the decisive moment in the history of the critical method. The humanism of the preceding age had had its stray impulses and its intuitions. It had gone no farther. Nothing is more characteristic than a passage from the *Essais* in which Montaigne justifies Tacitus for having reported miracles. It is, he says, the business of theologians and philosophers to debate the "common body of belief." Historians for their part have only to "relate" it, as given by their sources, "so that they render history rather as they receive it, than as they evaluate it." In other words, a philosophical criticism, resting upon a certain conception of the natural or divine order, is perfectly legitimate: and it is understood for the rest that Montaigne assumes responsibility neither for the miracles of Vespasian nor for a good many others. But he obviously does not really understand how it is possible to conduct an examination, specifically a historical examination, of evidence such as this. The doctrine of research was worked out in that seventeenth century whose true glory, although it is sometimes misplaced, belongs to its second half.

The men of that time were themselves aware of it. Between 1680 and 1690, it was a commonplace to denounce the "Pyrrhonism of history" as a momentary fad. "It is said," wrote Michel Levassor, commenting upon this term, "that rectitude of mind consists in not being too ready to believe and, on a number of occasions, in knowing how to doubt." The very word "criticism," which up to that time had connoted little more than a judgment of taste, is here passing to the almost new sense of a test of truth. At first, they ventured the term only apologetically, for "it is not entirely good usage," which is to say that the word still retained a technical flavor. Nevertheless, it gained steadily. Bossuet shied away from it. When he speaks of "our critical authors," we sense the shrugging of shoulders. Richard Simon, on the other hand, incorporated it into the title of almost all his works. The most circumspect were not misled by it. Indeed, what this word heralded was the discovery of a method of nearly universal applicability. According to Ellies du Pin, criticism was that "species of torch which lights our way down the darkened corridors of antiquity, enabling us to distinguish the true from the false." Bayle was even clearer: "M. Simon, in his new *Réponse*, has laid down a number of rules of criticism, which can be useful, not only for the understanding of the Scriptures, but also for the profitable reading of many other works."

Now, let us compare some birth dates: Papebroeck (who, if he was mistaken about the Merovingian charters, nevertheless, has a place among the founders of historical criticism), 1628; Mabillon, 1632; Richard Simon (whose works dominate the beginnings of Biblical exegesis), 1638. Outside the company of the scholars, properly speaking, let us add Spinoza—Spinoza of the *Tractatus Theologico-Politicus*, that pure masterpiece of philological and historical criticism—also 1632. In the strictest sense of the word, it is a generation whose outlines take shape before us with amazing clarity. But we must be more precise. This was the generation born at about the moment of the appearance of the *Discours de la Méthode.*

We must not call it a generation of Cartesians. Mabillon, for one, was a devout monk, naïvely orthodox, whose last-written work was a tract upon *La Mort Chrétienne.* It is doubtful that he had any very direct knowledge of the new philosophy which was then regarded with suspicion by so many pious folk, and it is still more doubtful that he would have found very much to approve in it even if he had had any chance glimmerings. Then again—whatever the perhaps unduly celebrated pages of Claude Bernard may seem to suggest—the truths of that mathematical sort of evidence for which Descartes's systematic doubt sought to pave the way present few common characteristics with those increasingly close approximations to truth which both historical criticism and laboratory science are content to define. But for a philosophy to impregnate an entire age, it is not necessary that it should act precisely in accordance with a prescribed formula nor that the majority of minds should come under its influence except by a sort of osmosis of which they are often only half aware. Like Cartesian "science," the criticism of historical evidence makes a *tabula rasa* of its beliefs. Like Cartesian science, too, it proceeds inexorably to knock out the props of antiquity only in order thereby to arrive at new certainties (or very strong probabilities), which are thenceforth duly proved. In other words, the idea supposes an almost total overturn of older conceptions of doubt. Up to that time, whether men considered that its sting might seem painful, or found in it an infinitely high-minded sweetness, they conceived of it only as a purely negative mental attitude, a mere vacuum. Thenceforth, they thought that, rationally conducted, doubt could become an instrument of knowledge. It is an idea which appeared at a very precise moment in the history of thought.

From that time, in short, the basic rules of the critical method were fixed. Their general significance was so little overlooked that among the subjects most frequently proposed for the competitive examinations in philosophy by the University of Paris in the eighteenth century was one having a curiously modern ring: "The testimony of men upon historical facts." This is certainly not to imply that the later generations did not greatly improve the tool of criticism. Above all, they widely generalized its use and extended its applications.

For a long time, critical techniques were practiced, at least with any consistency, almost exclusively by a handful of scholars, exigetes, and connoisseurs. Writers engaged in historical works of the high-flown sort scarcely bothered to familiarize themselves with such laboratory exercises, far too detailed for their taste, or even to take their results into account. Now, as Humboldt put it, it is never good for chemists to be afraid "of getting their hands wet." For history, the danger of a split between preparation and execution is double-edged. At the outset, it cruelly vitiates the great attempts at interpretation. Because of it, these not only fail in their primary duty of the patient quest for truth, but, deprived of that perpetual renewal, that constantly reborn surprise, which only the struggle with documents can supply, they inevitably lapse into a ceaseless oscillation between stereotyped themes imposed by routine. But technical work suffers no less. No longer guided from above, it risks being indefinitely marooned upon insignificant or poorly propounded questions. There is no waste more criminal than that of erudition running, as it were, in neutral gear, nor any pride more vainly misplaced than that in a tool valued as an end in itself.

The conscientious effort of the nineteenth century struggled valiantly against these perils. The German school, Renan, Fustel de Coulanges won for erudition its intellectual stature. The historian has been brought back to the workbench. But has the opposition been entirely won over? It would be optimistic to think so. Too often, the work of research still wanders aimlessly with no rational decision about where it is to be applied. Above all, criticism has not yet succeeded in winning over that wholehearted approval of "good men and true" (in the former sense of that phrase) whose backing, no doubt necessary to the moral health of any science, is more particularly indispensable to our own. If men, who are the object of our study, fail to understand us, how can we feel that we have accomplished more than half our mission?

In truth, perhaps, we have not fully accomplished it. The grim esoterism, in which even the best of us sometimes fall, the preponderance, in our current writing, of those dreary textbooks which bad teaching-concepts have put in place of true synthesis, the curious modesty which, as soon as we are outside the study, seems to forbid us to expose the honest groping of our methods before a profane public—all these bad habits, derived from an accumulation of contradictory prejudices, compromise the essential nobility of our cause. They conspire to surrender the mass of defenseless readers to the false brilliance of a bogus history, in which lack of seriousness, picturesque rubbish, and political prejudices are supposed to be redeemed by shameless self-assurance: thus, Maurras, Bainville, or Plekhanov affirm that which Fustel de Coulanges or Pirenne would have doubted. A misunderstanding between historical inquiry, such as it is or hopes to be, and the reading public unquestionably does exist. The great debate about footnotes is not the least significant ground upon which the two parties are engaged in their absurd duel.

For a great many scholars, the lower margin of the page exerts a fascination bordering upon mania. It is surely absurd to overcrowd these margins, as they do, with bibliographical references which might largely have been spared by a list drawn up at the beginning of the volume; and worse still, through sheer laziness, to relegate to them long explanations whose proper place was indicated in the main body of the text, so that the most useful part of these works must be looked for in the cellar. But when certain readers complain that a single note, strutting along by itself at the foot of the page, makes their heads swim, or when certain publishers claim that their customers, doubtless less hypersensitive in reality than they would have us believe, are tortured by the mere sight of a page thus disfigured, these æsthetes merely prove their imperviousness to the most elementary maxims of an intellectual ethic. For, apart from the free play of imagination, we have no right to make any assertion which cannot be verified and a historian who in using a document indicates the source as briefly as possible (that is, the means of finding it again) is only obeying a universal rule of honesty. Corrupted by dogma and myth, current opinion, even when it is least hostile to enlightenment, has lost the very taste for verification. On that day when, having first taken care not to discourage it with useless pedantry, we shall succeed in persuading the public to measure the value of a science in proportion to its willingness to make refutation easy, the forces of reason will achieve one of their most smashing victories. Our humble notes, our finicky little references, currently lampooned by many who do not understand them, are working toward that day.

. . .

The documents most frequently dealt with by the early scholars either represented themselves or were traditionally represented as belonging to a given author or a given period, and deliberately narrated such and such events. Did they speak the truth? Were the books ascribed to Moses really his? Were the charters bearing the name of Clovis authentic? How valid were the accounts of Exodus, or those of the *Lives of the Saints*? Such was the problem. Because history has tended to make more and more frequent use of unintentional evidence, it can no longer confine itself to weighing the explicit assertions of the documents. It has been necessary to wring from them further confessions which they had never intended to give.

Now, the critical rules, which proved themselves in the first instance, work equally well in the second. I have before me a batch of medieval charters. Some are dated; others are not. Wherever a date appears, it must be verified, for experience proves that it may be false. Wherever it is missing, it is important to establish it. In either case, the same course will be pursued. On the basis of the script (if it is an original), the style of the Latin, the institutions alluded to, and the general aspect of the enacting clause, I conjecture that a certain deed corresponds to the readily recognizable practices of French notaries about the year A.D. 1000. If it claims to belong to the Merovingian period, the fraud is exposed. If it has no date, one has been approximately established. Similarly the archæologist, whether he intends to classify prehistoric tools according to their age and civilization, or to track down false antiquities, examines, compares, and defines types and techniques of workmanship according to rules which are fundamentally the same in either case.

The historian is not—indeed, he is less and less—that rather grumpy examining magistrate whose unflattering portrait is easily imposed upon the unwary by certain introductory manuals. To be sure, he has not turned credulous. He knows that his witnesses can lie or be mistaken. But he is primarily interested in making them speak so that he may understand them. It is not the least admirable feature of the critical method that, without the least modification of its first principles, it has successfully continued to direct research towards this larger goal.

However, it would be wrongheaded to deny that incorrect evidence was not only the stimulus to the first efforts for a technique of truth, but continues to be the starting-point from which that technique must necessarily proceed in order to develop its analyses.

2. *In Pursuit of Fraud and Error*

Of all the poisons capable of vitiating a piece of evidence, the most virulent is deception.

This can take two forms. First of all, there is deceit as to the author and the date: forgery, in the legal sense of the word. Not all the letters published with Marie Antoinette's signature were written by her; there are some which were forged in the ninteenth century. The so-called tiara of Saïtphernès, sold to the

Louvre as a Scythio-Greek antiquity of the third century B.C., had been engraved at Odessa in 1895. Secondly, there is misrepresentation of the facts. In the *Commentaries,* whose authorship is incontestible, Cæsar has consciously distorted or omitted a great deal. The statue displayed at St. Denis as representing Philip the Bold is, indeed, the funerary figure of that king, as it was executed after his death; but everything suggests that the sculptor simply reproduced a conventional model which is a portrait in name only.

Now, these two aspects of fraud raise entirely distinct problems, with quite separate solutions.

Certainly, the majority of those writings which bear a forged name falsify their contents as well. The Protocols of the Elders of Zion, apart from the fact that they were not written by the Elders of Zion, made the widest possible departures from the substance of the truth. If an alleged charter of Charlemagne should prove, upon examination, to have been forged two or three centuries later, the chances are that the acts of generosity which it attributes to the Emperor are equally fictitious. Nevertheless, even this cannot be taken for granted, for some deeds have been forged with the sole purpose of repeating the dispositions of entirely authentic papers which have been lost. In exceptional cases, then, a forgery may speak the truth.

Inversely, it should be superfluous to recall that that evidence which is entirely above suspicion as to its avowed origin is not, for that reason, necessarily truthful. However, scholars take such pains to weigh a document before accepting it as authentic that afterwards they sometimes lack the stamina to criticize its contents. Moreover, they are particularly loath to doubt those writings which are sanctioned by impressive legal guarantees, such as actions of official authority or even private contracts. Yet neither deserves much respect. On April 21, 1834, prior to the prosecution of the secret societies, Thiers wrote to the prefect of the lower Rhine: "I advise you to take the greatest care to furnish your share of documents for the great forthcoming investigations. The correspondence of all anarchists, the intimate connections between events in Paris, Lyons, Strassburg, and, in a word, the existence of a vast conspiracy embracing the whole of France—all this must be made entirely clear." Unquestionably, here is a well-prepared official documentation! As for duly sealed and dated charters, the least experience of the present is enough to dispel all illusions about them. Everybody knows that the most regularly established and notarized deeds teem with intentional inaccuracies, and I remember recently having been ordered to antedate my signature at the foot of a report demanded by one of the great government services of the state. Our ancestors were not more fastidious in this respect. "Promulgated upon such and such a day in such and such a place," they say at the bottom of royal charters. But if you consult the accounts of the king's travels, you will see more than once that, upon the specified date, he was actually several leagues away. Innumerable acts of enfranchisement of serfs, which no one who is not mad would dream of arguing as forgeries, are asserted to derive from pure charity, even though we can place beside them the actual bill paid for emancipation.

But to establish the fact of forgery is not enough. It is further necessary to discover its motivations, if only as an aid to tracking it down. So long as there is any doubt about its origins, there is something in it which defies analysis and which is, therefore, only half proved. Above all, a fraud is, in its way, a piece of evidence. Merely to prove that the famous charter of Charlemagne to the church at Aix-la-Chapelle is not authentic is to avoid error, but not to acquire knowledge. On the other hand, should we succeed in proving that the forgery was committed by the followers of Frederick Barbarossa, and that it was designed to implement dreams of imperial grandeur, we open new vistas upon the vast perspectives of history. Here, then, we see criticism seeking out the impostor behind the imposture. In other words, we see it conforming to the basic motto of history, by seeking out man.

It would be puerile to pretend to enumerate the infinite variety of reasons which can lead to lying. But the historian, who tends naturally to overintellectualize mankind, would do well to remember that all of these reasons are not in fact reasonable. With certain people, lying (although it is itself generally joined to a compound of egotism and suppressed desire) is almost, as André Gide put it, a "gratuitous act." The German savant who took such great pains to write, in excellent Greek, an oriental history whose authorship he attributed to the fictitious Sanchoniathon, might, with less effort, have acquired a respectable reputation as a Hellenist. François Lenormant, the son of a member of the Institute and himself later called to join that honorable company, began his career at seventeen by deceiving his own father with the fraudulent discovery at La Chapelle Saint-Eloi of inscriptions carved entirely by his own hand; even when old and laden with honors, his last masterly coup was said to have been the publicizing as Greek originals of a number of commonplace prehistoric relics which he had simply gathered up from the French countryside.

Now, there have been mythomaniac epochs, as well as individuals with a passion for lying. Such were the preromantic or romantic generations toward the end of the eighteenth and beginning of the nineteenth century. There were the pseudo-Celtic poems attributed to Ossian, the epic poems and ballads written in what Chatterton believed was Old English, the allegedly medieval poetry of Clothilde of Surville, the Breton songs devised by Villemarqué, songs said to have been translated from Croatian by Mérimée, the heroic Czech songs from the manuscript of Kravoli-Dvor, and others too numerous to mention. During these decades, it was as if a vast symphony of deception resounded from one end of Europe to the other. The Middle Ages, especially from the eighth to the twelfth century, presents another example of this mass epidemic. Certainly, the majority of the false charters, capitularies, and pontifical decrees which were then forged in such great numbers were designed to serve some selfish interest. To secure disputed property to a church, to support the authority of the Roman See, to defend the monks from the Bishop, the bishops from the metropolitans, the Pope from the temporal rulers, or the Emperor from the Pope—such were the sole objectives of the forgers. Their common characteristic is that persons of incontestible piety and even of integrity did not hesitate to put their hands to these forgeries. Obviously, such forgeries were hardly offensive to public morality. As for plagiarism, it was at this time universally regarded as the most innocent act in the world. Annalists and hagiographers shamelessly appropriated entire passages from the writings of earlier authors. Although so different in other respects, there is nothing less "futuristic" than these two societies. The Middle Ages knew no other foundation for either its faith or its laws than the teachings of its ancestors. Romanticism wished to steep itself in the living spring of the primitive, as well as in that of the popular. So it was that the periods which were the most bound by tradition were also those which took the greatest liberties with their true heritage. It is as if, in a curious compensation for an irresistible creative urge, they were naturally led, by the sheer force of their veneration of the past, to invent it.

In the month of July 1857, Michel Chasles, the mathematician, presented to the Academy of Science an entire collection of unpublished letters of Pascal, which had been sold to him by his regular dealer, the brilliant forger Vrain-Lucas. From these it appeared that the author of the *Provinciales* had formulated the principle of gravitation prior to Newton. This amazed a certain English savant. How was it possible to explain, he asked, in effect, that these writings took note of astronomical measurements made many years after Pascal's death, and of which even Newton had no knowledge until after the publication of the first articles of his work? Vrain-Lucas was not the man to be troubled by such a mere trifle. He again sat down to his desk, and, before long, fortified by his painstaking labors, Chasles was able to produce some new "originals." This time, Galileo was the signer and Pascal the recipient. The mystery was explained as follows: the illustrious astronomer had provided the observations and Pascal the calculations. The whole correspondence had been secret on both sides. It is true that Pascal was only eighteen at the death of Galileo. But what of that? It was but another reason to admire the precocity of his genius.

Nevertheless, the indefatigable objector noted still another peculiarity: in one of the letters, dated 1641, Galileo complains that he cannot write without greatly tiring his eyes. Now, do we not know that he had actually been stone blind since the close of 1637? "I beg your pardon," replied the good Chasles after a little; "I admit that, until now, everyone had believed in that blindness. But they were quite mistaken. For, it so happens that I can now add to the discussion a decisive paper which will refute this universal error. On December 2, 1641, another Italian scholar informed Pascal that Galileo, whose sight had unquestionably been failing for several years, had just lost it entirely."

Certainly, not all forgers have displayed as much imagination as Vrain-Lucas; nor all dupes so much gullibility as his pitiable victim; but the experience of life teaches, and that of history confirms, that any offense against the truth is like a net and that almost inevitably every lie drags in its train many others, summoned to lend it a semblance of mutual support. That is why so many famous forgeries occur in clusters. In the false privileges of the See of Canterbury, in the false privileges of the Duchy of Austria—signed by so many great sovereigns, from Julius Cæsar to Frederick Barbarossa—and in the forgeries of the Dreyfus affair which spread like a genealogical table (and I cite but a few examples), we seem to perceive a growing gangrene. By its very nature, one fraud begets another.

Finally, there is a more insidious form of deception. In place of blunt, forthright, and, I might almost say, honest untruths, there are the sly alterations: interpolations in authentic charters or the embroidering of imaginary details upon the roughly trustworthy scheme of a narrative. Interpolations are generally founded on self-interest. Embroidery is frequently for the purpose of embellishment. The havoc wrought upon ancient or medieval historiography by a mistaken æsthetic sense has often been exposed. Its role in our press is perhaps no less important. The most unpretentious of our newspapermen intentionally presents his characters, even at the cost of the truth, in accordance with a rhetorical tradition whose glamor our age has not outworn, and our editorial staffs include more disciples of Aristotle and Quintilian than is generally believed.

Certain technical conditions themselves seem to favor these distortions. In 1917, when the spy, Bolo, was condemned, one daily is said to have published the account of his execution on April 6. In reality, although it was originally set for that date, it did not actually take place until eleven days later. The journalist had set up his "copy" beforehand; convinced that the event would take place upon the day anticipated, he deemed it useless to verify it. I do not know what the anecdote may be worth. Certainly, such awkward mistakes are the exception, but it is not at all an improbable assumption that, since time is of the essence in delivering the copy, the reports of anticipated events are often prepared in advance for the sake of expediency. Almost always, we may be sure, the sketch will be changed on all important points, if that seems advisable after observation; on the other hand, it may be doubted that very many alterations are made in the supplementary details which are deemed necessary for color and which nobody cares to verify. At least, that is how it seems to a layman. It is to be wished that a professional man would supply us with genuine enlightenment on the subject. Unfortunately, the press has not yet found its Mabillon. Certainly, submission to a rather antiquated code of literary propriety, deference to a stereotyped psychology, and the rage for the picturesque are nowhere near to losing their place as causes of fabrication.

If only because of the ease with which chance may transform the sincerest blunder into a lie, there are many gradations from sham, pure and simple, to the entirely unintentional error. The act of inventing a lie presupposes an effort which is distasteful to the mental inertia common to the majority of men. It is much easier to accept with complacency an illusion, at first spontaneous, which gratifies the interest of the moment.

Take the famous case of "the airplane of Nuremberg." Although the fact has never been definitely established, it seems highly probable that a French commercial plane flew over the city several days prior to the declaration of war. It is probable that it was taken for a military plane. It is not improbable that, in a population already a prey to the specter of the forthcoming conflict, there were spread rumors of bombs dropped here and there. Nevertheless, it is certain that none were dropped; that the officials of the German government possessed every means of suppressing the false rumor; and hence that, in welcoming it without verification, to use it as a motive for war, they clearly lied. But they did so without inventing anything, and even, perhaps, without being clearly conscious of their deception at the outset. The absurd rumor was believed, because it was useful to believe it. Of all the types of deception, not the least frequent is that which we impose upon ourselves, and the word "sincerity" has so broad a meaning that it cannot be used without admitting a great many shadings.

It is no less true that many witnesses deceive themselves in all good faith. The time is now ripe for the historian to profit from the precious results of those observations from life which in the last few decades have provided the tools of a nearly new discipline: the psychology of evidence. In so far as they involve our studies, these discoveries seem to be essentially as follows.

If we are to believe William of St. Thierry, his friend and disciple, St. Bernard, was very surprised to learn one day that the chapel where he had daily attended divine service as a young monk opened onto the chevet by three windows, although he had always imagined that it had had only one. The hagiographer expresses astonishment and admiration at this trait, for does not such a detachment from the things of this world betoken a perfect servant of God? Unquestionably, Bernard appears really to have been uncommonly absent-minded—at least if it is true, as is also related, that once later, he traveled along the shores of Lake Geneva for an entire day without being aware of it. Nevertheless, there is plenty of proof to show that it is not necessary to be one of the foremost mystics to be grossly mistaken about those realities which should seemingly be the best known to us. In the course of famous experiments at Geneva, the students of Professor Claparède proved themselves as incapable of accurately describing the entrance hall of their university as did the doctor "according to the honeyed word" the church of his monastery. The truth is that the majority of minds are but mediocre recording-cameras of the surrounding world. Add that, since evidence, strictly speaking, is no more than the expression of remembrance, the first errors of perception run the constant risk of being entangled with the errors of memory, that loose, that "slippery" memory, denounced long ago by one of our old jurists.

For certain minds, inaccuracy possesses a truly pathological fascination—would it be too irreverent to call this psychosis "Lamartine's disease"? At any rate, we all know that its victims are not ordinarily the most reluctant to make positive statements. But if this is so of more or less dubious witnesses, experience shows that there are no witnesses whose statements are equally reliable on all subjects and under all circumstances. There is no reliable witness in the absolute sense. There is only more or less reliable testimony. Two principal sorts of circumstances impair the accuracy of perception of even the most gifted person. The first depends upon the condition of the observer at the time—such, for example, as his fatigue or emotion—the second upon the degree of his attention. With few exceptions, we see and really understand only that to which we devote our particular concentration. If a physician visits a sickbed, I am more willing to credit his report about the appearance of the patient whom he has carefully examined, than about the furniture of the room, to which he has probably given only a passing glance. That is why, contrary to a common prejudice, the most familiar objects—in the case of St. Bernard, the chapel at Citeaux—are usually those of which it is most difficult to get an accurate description, for familiarity almost inevitably breeds indifference.

Now, a great many historical events can have been observed only in moments of violent emotional confusion, or by witnesses whose attention, whether attracted too late in the event of surprise, or preoccupied by the need for immediate action, was incapable of sufficient concentration upon those features in which historians have reason to be most interested today. Certain examples are notorious. Whence came the first shot which precipitated the riot in front of the Office of Foreign Affairs on February 25, 1848—and from which in its turn the revolution was to result? Did it come from the troops or from the crowd? In all likelihood we shall never know. How then can we now take seriously the full-blown descriptive passages of the chroniclers, with their detailed portrayals of dress, movements, ceremonies, and feats in battle? By what stubborn habit of mind are we to preserve the least illusion of the accuracy of all this stuff, the delight of the small fry of romantic historians, when we see around us no one with the ability to remember correctly in their entirety those details of the kind which are naïvely sought for in the ancient authors? At best, these tableaux give us the setting of the action, as contemporaries of the writer imagined it should have been. That is extremely informative, but it is not the sort of information which the lovers of the picturesque generally desire from their sources.

However, it is advisable to understand what conclusions about the nature of our studies are implied by these remarks, which are pessimistic perhaps in appearance only. They do not affect the fundamental structure of the past. The words of Bayle remain forever true. "No valid objection will ever be raised to the fact that Cæsar defeated Pompey. On whatever grounds we may choose to argue it, there is hardly anything more unshakeable than this proposition: Cæsar and Pompey existed. They were not merely in the minds of those who wrote their lives." It is true that, if there were no certainty except for a few facts of this type devoid of explanation, history would be reduced to a series of rough notations without much intellectual value. Happily, such is not the case. It is only the most immediately antecedent causes which are frequently rendered uncertain by the psychology of evidence. A great event can be compared to an explosion. Under exactly what conditions was produced the last molecular shock, indispensable for the expansion of the gas? We must often resign ourselves to ignorance. This is no doubt regrettable, but what of the chemists? Their position is not always much better. Nevertheless, the composition of the explosive mixture remains perfectly susceptible of analysis. The revolution of 1848, despite the fact that, by a strange aberration, certain historians have thought to make it the archetype of the fortuitous event, was a movement clearly determined by a great number of extremely diverse and dynamic factors, which had been preparing its way for a long time and which in fact enabled a Tocqueville to foresee it. As for the fusillade on the Boulevard de Capucines, what was that but the last little spark?

Moreover, we shall see that all too often the immediate causes escape our witnesses', and hence our own, observation. They embody that privileged part of history which is unforeseeable, "accidental." We may easily console ourselves if the flimsiness of evidence conceals them from our subtlest instruments. Even if they were better known, their connection with the great causal chains of evolution would represent that residue of fallacy which our science will never eliminate, and which it has no right even to pretend to eliminate. As for the hidden causes of human destiny, the fluctuations in mental or emotional climate, the changes in techniques, and the variations in the social or economic structure, our witnesses will hardly be subject to the frailty of instantaneous perception. It is a happy coincidence, long ago glimpsed by Voltaire, that what is most profound in history may also be the most certain.

. . .

The faculty of observation is as variable among societies as among individuals. Certain epochs show themselves more wanting in this respect than others. For example, however feeble the understanding of numbers among the majority of men today, it is no longer so universally defective as among the medieval annalists. Our perception, like our civilization, is saturated with mathematics. Were errors of testimony due solely to failings of the senses or of attention, the historian would have little choice but to abandon the subject to the psychologist. But, beyond common mental slips, there are many errors that derive from a particular social climate. Such errors often assume a documentary value in their turn.

In September 1917, the infantry regiment to which I belonged held the trenches of the Chemin des Dames to the north of the little town of Braisne. In one attack, we took a prisoner. He was a reservist, a wholesale merchant by trade, and originally from Bremen on the Weser. Shortly thereafter, a curious tale came up from behind the lines. "German espionage!" our well-informed comrades said, in effect. "What a marvel it is! We find one of their outposts in the heart of France. Astounding! A merchant stationed in peacetime Braisne." [1] We must beware of explaining the story too simply. To blame it all on an error of hearing is inexact. The error was not merely in hearing but in understanding. Because the name

[1] Note that Brême, the French for Bremen, sounds very much like Braisne in rapid speech.

was generally unfamiliar, it had not caught the attention. By a natural mental quirk, a familiar name was substituted in its place. Furthermore, a second and equally unconscious interpretation was at work in the first. The idea of German cunning, frequently all too true, had been popularized by innumerable anecdotes, highly gratifying to the romantic sensibilities of the masses. The substitution of Braisne for Bremen accorded too well with this obsession not to have been spread, as it were, spontaneously.

Now, such is the case with a great number of the distortions of evidence. Nearly always, the nature of the error is determined in advance. More particularly, it does not spread, it does not take on life, unless it harmonizes with the prejudices of public opinion. It then becomes as a mirror in which the collective consciousness surveys its own features. On the fronts of a great many Belgian houses, there are narrow apertures designed to help the plasterers in setting up their scaffolding; the German soldiers in 1914 would never have envisioned these innocent contrivances of the masons as so many loopholes prepared for snipers, if their imaginations had not long been deranged by the fear of guerrillas. Clouds have not changed their shapes since the Middle Ages, yet we no longer see in them either magical swords or miraculous crosses. The tail of the comet sighted by the great Ambroise Paré was probably very little different from those which occasionally sweep across our skies. Yet, he thought he saw in it a full suit of curious armor. Compliance with universal prejudice had bested the habitual accuracy of his gaze; and his testimony, like that of so many others, tells us not what he actually saw but what his age thought it natural to see.

However, for the error of a single witness to become that of many men, for an inaccurate observation to be transformed into a false rumor, social conditions must be such as to favor its circulation. Certainly not all types of society are equally auspicious. The extraordinary disturbances of collective life in our time include many remarkable experiences in this regard. Those of the present moment are too close to us to permit of exact analysis as yet. The war of 1914–18 offers a greater perspective.

Everyone knows how productive of false news these four years proved to be, particularly among the combat troops. It is their formation in the very extraordinary society of the trenches which is the most interesting to study.

The role of propaganda and censorship was considerable, but in a way exactly the reverse of what the creators of these institutions expected of them. As one witness very neatly remarked: "The prevailing opinion in the trenches was that anything might be true, except what was printed." The men put no faith in newspapers, and scarcely more in letters, for these, besides arriving irregularly, were thought to be heavily censored. From this there arose a prodigious renewal of oral tradition, the ancient mother of myths and legends. Wiping out bygone centuries by a daring stroke, beyond the wildest dream of the boldest experimenters, governments reduced the front-line soldier to the means of information and the mental state of olden times before journals, before news sheets, before books.

Rumors did not ordinarily originate on the firing-line. There, the little groups were too isolated from one another. The soldier could not move about except under orders; most frequently, moreover, he did so only at the risk of his life. Occasionally, intermittent travelers went the rounds: liaison officers, artillery observers, telephone communications men repairing their lines. These notable personages scarcely associated with the common soldier. But there were also regular communications of far more importance. They were made necessary by the demand for sustenance. The *agoræ* of this little world of dugouts and observation posts were the field kitchens. There, once or twice a day, the carriers from the various points of the sector came together, met again, and chatted amongst themselves or with the cooks. The latter knew a great deal, for, situated on the crossroads of all units, they had the additional and rare privilege of exchanging a few words daily with the drivers of the regimental service corps, fortunate men who were quartered in the vicinity of staff headquarters. Thus, for a moment, around fires in the open air or the grates of the field kitchens, there were momentary contacts among very dissimilar groups. Then the fatigue parties, moving off by the trails and communication trenches, brought to the most forward parts of the front, along with their camp kettles, this mass of intelligence true or false, almost always distorted in every circumstance and ready for further elaboration there. On the tactical maps, a little behind those interlacing lines which designate the forward positions, it would be possible to hatch in a continuous strip which would be the myth-making zone.

Now, history has known more than one society governed, on the whole, by analogous conditions, but with this difference: that instead of being the passing effect of an entirely exceptional crisis they here represent the normal texture of life. Here also, almost the only effective means of transmission is oral. Here too, the liaison between widely separated elements is carried on almost exclusively by specialized intermediaries or at definite points of juncture. Peddlars, jugglers, pilgrims, beggars take the place of the little fellows wandering through the communication trenches. The regular meetings occur at markets or on the occasion of religious holidays, as, for example, during the high Middle Ages. Based on information gained from cross-questioning passers-by, monastic chronicles greatly resemble the notebooks which our supply corporals could have kept if they had had the desire. Such societies have always been excellent culture media for false news. Frequent contacts among men make it easy to compare divergent stories. They stimulate the critical sense. On the other hand, we have faith in that narrator who, at rare intervals, brings us distant rumors over a difficult road.

3. *Toward a Logic of the Critical Method*

Criticism of testimony, since it deals with psychic realities, will always remain a subtle art. There is no recipe for it. However, it is also a rational art, which depends on methodical use of certain basic mental processes. In a word, it has a dialectic of its own which we ought to try to define.

Let us suppose that only one object is left from a lost civilization, and moreover that the conditions of its discovery forbid placing it even in a non-human context, such as geological sedimentation. (For inanimate nature may play its part in such research.) It would be entirely impossible to date this unique vestige, or even to render a verdict as to its authenticity. In fact, we can never establish a date, we can never verify, and, in short, we can never interpret a document except by inserting it into a chronological series or a synchronous whole. It was by comparing Merovingian charters, now with each other, now with other texts of a different nature and time, that Mabillon founded the science of diplomatics. It was the collation of the stories of the Gospel which gave rise to Biblical exegesis. At the bottom of nearly all criticism there is a problem of comparison.

But the outcome of this comparison has nothing of

the automatic about it. Of necessity, it ends by revealing similarities and differences. Now, depending upon the circumstances, agreement of one testimony with other testimonies may lead to opposite conclusions.

To begin with, we must first consider the elementary matter of narrative. In the *Memoirs* which have thrilled so many young hearts, Marbot relates, with a great multiplicity of detail, a feat of courage of which he makes himself the hero: according to him, on the night of May 7, 1809, he crossed the raging torrents of the Danube, which was then in full flood, in order to free some prisoners of the Austrians on the other side. How are we to verify the anecdote? We must summon the other evidences to the rescue. We possess the orders, the records of march, and the reports of the opposing armies. They attest that, upon the famous night, the Austrian corps whose bivouac Marbot claimed to have located on the left bank was still on the opposite side. In another connection, it is evident from the *Correspondence* of Napoleon himself that, on May 8, the high waters had not begun. Finally, we have discovered a petition for promotion drawn up by Marbot in person on June 30, 1809. Among the claims he here set forth, he breathed not a word about his supposed exploit of the preceding month. On one side, then, we have the *Memoirs*; on the other, a whole batch of documents which belie them. We must now decide between these conflicting witnesses. Which alternative will be judged the most likely: that the general staff and the Emperor himself were simultaneously mistaken (unless, God only knows why, they had knowingly falsified reality) and that the Marbot of 1809, desperately eager for advancement, had erred through false modesty, or that, much later, the old warrior, whose boasts are notorious in other connections, had won another bout with the truth? Surely no one will hesitate. The *Memoirs* have lied again.

Here, then, the statement of a disagreement has destroyed one of the conflicting testimonies. One of them had to yield. The most universal of logical postulates demanded such an outcome. The principle of contradiction pitilessly denies that an event can be and not be at the same time. There are in the world scholars whose good nature has worn itself out in seeking a middle ground between antagonistic statements. They are like the little chap who, asked for the square of the number two, when one neighbor whispered "four" and the other "eight," thought he had hit the mark in answering "six."

It then remained for us to choose which evidence should be rejected and which retained. It was decided by a psychological analysis: the supposed reasons for truthfulness, for deceit, and for error were weighed for all the witnesses in turn. In this particular case, it was found that this appraisal assumed the character of nearly absolute evidence. It would unfailingly show a much larger coefficient of uncertainty under other circumstances. Conclusions which are founded upon a delicate imputation of motive fall upon a graduated scale from the infinitely probable to the barely credible.

But now here are some examples of another sort.

A charter which claims to be of the twelfth century is written on paper, whereas all the originals of that period hitherto recovered are on parchment; the shape of the letters here seems very different from the forms which we see in other documents of the same time; the language abounds in words and tricks of style entirely foreign to their practice. Or, again, the edge of a tool, supposed to be paleolithic, betrays processes of workmanship which, according to our knowledge, were used only in much more recent times. We conclude that the charter and the tool are forgeries. As before, the disagreement is damning, but for reasons of a very different nature.

This time, the line of argument is that within a single generation of the same society there prevails a similarity of custom and technique too strong to permit any person to deviate sensibly from the common practice. We take for granted that any Frenchman of the time of Louis VII drew his downstrokes in pretty much the same way as his contemporaries,[2] that he

[2] In my youth, I heard a very illustrious scholar, who was director of the École des Chartes, tell us rather haughtily: "I date the handwriting of a manuscript within twenty years without a mistake." He overlooked only one thing. Many men and many scribes live more than forty years—and if handwritings sometimes change with age, it is rare for them to adapt themselves to the new handwritings

expressed himself in pretty much the same terms and that he made use of the same materials. Likewise, we assume that if a craftsman of the Magdalenian tribe had invented a mechanical saw to cut out his arrowheads, his comrades would have used it as he did. In brief, the postulate in this case is of a sociological order.

Nevertheless, the resemblance ought not to be too strong. It would then cease to support the case. On the contrary, it would weaken it.

Anyone who took part in the battle of Waterloo knew that Napoleon was beaten. Any witness so singular as to deny the defeat we should regard as a liar. Moreover, if we confine ourselves to the simple, blunt statement, there are not very many different ways of saying that Napoleon was beaten at Waterloo. But should two witnesses describe the battle in exactly the same language or, despite a certain variation of phrasing, with exactly the same details, we should unhesitatingly conclude that one of them had copied the other or that both had copied a common model. In effect, our reason refuses to admit that two observers, necessarily posted at different parts of the field and endowed with unequal powers of attention, could have noted the same episodes, detail for detail; that two writers, working independently of one another, should

about them. About 1200, there must have been some sextagenarian scribes who still wrote as they had been taught about 1150. In fact, the history of handwriting is curiously behind that of language. It is waiting for its Diez—or its Meillet.

accidentally have chosen from among the innumerable words of the French language the same terms, similarly arranged, in order to narrate the same things. If the two accounts claim to have been taken directly from reality, then at least one of them must be lying.

Again, let us consider two battle scenes sculptured in stone upon two ancient monuments. They refer to different campaigns, yet they are depicted with nearly the same details. The archæologist would say: "Unless both artists were satisfied with reproducing a traditional design, one has certainly plagiarized from the other." It matters little that the combats had been separated by but a short interval, that perhaps they involved adversaries from the same peoples—Egyptians against Hittites, Assur against Elam. We rebel at the thought that, considering the immense variety of human positions, two distinct actions at different moments could have exactly repeated the same gestures. As evidence of the military annals which they pretend to record, at least one, if not both of these representations, is, strictly speaking, a fraud.

Thus, criticism oscillates between two extremes: the similarity which vindicates and that which discredits. This is because there is a limit to coincidence, and social unity is made up of links which are, on the whole, rather weak. In other words, we estimate that the universe and society possess sufficient uniformity to exclude the possibility of overly pronounced deviations. But, as we picture it to ourselves, this uniformity is confined to some very general characteristics. It includes, we think upon delving further into reality, a number of possible combinations so nearly infinite that their spontaneous repetition is inconceivable: there must be a voluntary act of imitation. And so, to add it all up, the criticism of evidence relies upon an instinctive metaphysics of the similar and the dissimilar, of the one and the many.

Once having set up the hypothesis of a copy, we must establish the direction of the influence. In each case, we must ask whether the two documents have borrowed from a common source. If, on the other hand, we suppose one of them to be original, to which shall we accord the honor of this title? Sometimes the answer is provided by external criteria, such as the relative dates, if these can be established. Failing these aids, psychological analysis, making use of the internal characteristics of the objects or texts, again comes into its own.

It goes without saying that this conforms to no mechanical rules. For example, is it necessary, as certain scholars seem to think, to lay down the principle that adapters are continually adding new fantasies, so that the odds are always that the most restrained and least improbable text is the oldest? Sometimes this is true. The number of enemies fallen under the blows of an Assyrian king are seen to swell enormously from inscription to inscription. But sometimes, too, common sense protests. The most fabulous of the *Passions* of St. George is the first in date; taking up the old account afterward, the successive biographers have sacrificed, one after the other, those features whose unrestrained fantasy shocked them. There are many different ways of imitating. They vary with the individual and, sometimes, with the vogue common to a generation. Like all other mental attitudes, they cannot be taken for granted on the pretext that they seem natural to us.

Fortunately, the plagiarists are often betrayed by their own blunders. When they do not understand their model, their misinterpretation proclaims the imposture. If they attempt to disguise their borrowings, the awkwardness of their stratagem betrays them. I knew a schoolboy, who, riveting his gaze upon his neighbor's paper during a written examination, painstakingly wrote down the sentences in reverse. With high cunning he changed the subjects to predicates and the actives to passives. He succeeded only in providing his professor with an excellent example of historical criticism.

To unmask an imitation is to reduce two or more witnesses to only one. Two of Marbot's contemporaries, the Count de Ségur and General Pelet, have given accounts of the supposed crossing of the Danube which are analogous to his own. But Ségur came after Pelet. He had read him. He did little more than to copy him. As for Pelet, he did indeed write before Marbot; but he was his friend, and, doubtless, he had often heard him recall his fictitious feats of valor—for, in deceiving his friends, the indefatigable braggart was intentionally preparing to mystify posterity. Since his seeming corroborators were only repeating his words, Marbot is then left really as our sole authority. When Livy repeats Polybius, even with embellishments, it is Polybius who is our sole authority. And when Einhard, while pretending to describe Charlemagne for us, plagiarizes the portrait of Augustus by Suetonius, we have really no witness left at all.

Finally, there are times when a prompter, who does not wish to identify himself, is hiding behind the self-styled witness. In studying the trial of the Templars, H. C. Lea observed that whenever two defendants of two different houses were examined by the same inquisitor they invariably confessed to the same atrocities and the same blasphemies. On the other hand, if defendants from the same house were questioned by different inquisitors, their confessions ceased to agree. The obvious conclusion is that the judge dictated the answers. I imagine that the annals of the judiciary might provide other examples of this peculiarity.

Surely, nowhere in the field of critical reasoning does the part played by what might be termed limited similarity appear in a more curious light than in one of the newest applications of method: statistical criticism.

Let us suppose that I have made a study of prices between two set dates in a tightly knit society in which there is active exchange. Later a second worker, and then a third, undertake the same research, but with the help of data differing from both mine and each other's: other account books, other market prices. Each of us separately draws up his annual averages, graphs, and index numbers on a common base. The three curves nearly coincide. We should conclude that each of them furnishes a more or less exact picture of the trend. Why?

The reason is not solely that in a homogeneous economic milieu large-scale price fluctuations must necessarily conform to a reasonably uniform rhythm. No doubt, this consideration would be enough to throw suspicion upon drastically divergent curves, but it is not enough to assure us that among all the possible plottings, that curve upon which the three graphs agreed must necessarily be the true one, simply because they agreed. Three scales whose balances are similarly false will give the same reading, and that reading will be false. Here, all reasoning relies upon an analysis of the mechanics of error. None of the three price lists could be held to be free of errors of detail. In statistical matters, they are nearly inevitable. Even if we disregard the personal mistakes of the investigator (and which of us has not blundered frightfully in the appalling maze of ancient weights and measures?), however miraculously attentive we imagine his research, there will always remain the pitfalls within the documents themselves. Certain prices may have been listed inaccurately, either through inadvertence or bad faith; others may be exceptional—prices for friends or, conversely, prices for fools. All of these are very apt to upset the averages. Lists recording average prices prevailing at the market were not always prepared with perfect care. Over a vast number of prices, however, these errors compensate for each other, for it would be extremely unlikely that they should all tend in the same direction. If, then, results attained by the use of different data are confirmed by their agreement, it is basically because agreement in the errors of the data—the oversights, the petty details, and the petty favors—seems inconceivable to us. The irreducible diversity in the evidence leads us to conclude that what there is of final agreement must derive from a reality whose fundamental unity, in this case, was beyond a doubt.

The reagents for the testing of evidence should not be roughly handled. Nearly all the rational principles, nearly all the experiences which guide the tests, if pushed far enough, reach their limits in contrary principles or experiences. Like any self-respecting logic, historical criticism has its contradictions or, at least, its paradoxes.

We have seen that, for a piece of evidence to be recognized as authentic, method demands that it show a certain correspondence to the allied evidences. Were we to apply this precept literally to the letter, however, what would become of discovery? For to speak of discovery is also to speak of surprise and dissimilarity. A science which restricted itself to stating that everything invariably happens according to expectation would hardly be either profitable or amusing. Up to now, there have been found no charters drafted in French (instead of Latin, as previously) which are anterior to 1204. Let us imagine that, tomorrow, a scholar should bring forward a French charter dated 1180. Are we to conclude that the document is fraudulent, or that our knowledge had been insufficient?

A seeming contradiction between a new piece of evidence and its surroundings may well have its source only in a temporary defect in our knowledge. But there are sometimes genuine disagreements in the objects themselves. Social uniformity is not so powerful as to be inescapable for certain individuals or small groups. Under the pretext that Pascal did not write like Arnauld, or that Cézanne did not paint like Bouguereau, are we to refuse to admit the recognized dates of the *Provinciales* or the *Montagne Ste. Victoire*? Are we to infer that the oldest bronze tools are forgeries, because most contemporary strata contain only stone tools?

These false conclusions are not at all imaginary, and one could make a long list of facts which scholarly routine first denied because they were surprising—from the Egyptian zoolatry with which Voltaire was so highly amused, down to the Roman remains of the tertiary era. On closer inspection, however, the methodological paradox is only on the surface. The principle of reasoning from similarity loses none of its force. It is only essential that a more exact analysis should distinguish the range of possible divergence, while making clear the necessary points of similitude.

For all individual originality has its limits. The style of Pascal belongs to him alone; but his grammar and the stock of his vocabulary belong to his time. Though it employs an unusual language, our hypothetical charter of 1180 is not impossibly different from other previously known charters of the same date. It can be judged acceptable if its French conforms in general to the state of the language as known from the literary texts of that epoch, and if the institutions which it mentions correspond to those of its time.

Moreover, rightly understood, critical comparison is not content to collate evidences from the same plane of time. A human phenomenon is always linked to a chain which spans the ages. On the day when a new Vrain-Lucas, throwing a handful of autographs upon the table of the Academy, shall pretend to prove that Pascal invented general relativity before Einstein, we may assume in advance that the papers will be forged. It is not that Pascal could not have discovered what his contemporaries did not. But the theory of relativity took its point of departure from a long anterior development of mathematical speculation. However great he may be, no man can dispense with the labor of generations by the sheer force of his genius. When, on the contrary, certain scholars, confronted with the first discoveries of paleolithic painting, contested their authenticity or date on the pretext that such an art could not have flourished and then vanished, these skeptics reasoned ill: chains may break, and civilizations may die.

As Father Delehaye writes, in substance, anyone reading that the church observes a holiday for two of its servants both of whom died in Italy on the very same day, that the conversion of each was brought about by the reading of the Lives of the Saints, that each founded a religious order dedicated to the same patron, and finally that both of these orders were suppressed by popes bearing the same name—anyone reading all this would be tempted to assert that a single individual, duplicated through error, had been entered in the martyrology under two different names. Nevertheless, it is quite true that, similarly converted to the religious life by the example of saintly biographies, St. John Colombini established the Order of Jesuates and Ignatius Loyola that of the Jesuits; that both of them died on July 31, the former near Siena in 1367, the latter at Rome in 1556; that the Jesuates were dissolved by Pope Clement IX and the Jesuits by Clement XIV. If the example is stimulating, it is certainly not unique. Should some future cataclysm destroy all but the bare outlines of the philosophical works of the past centuries, what a crowd of conscientious doubts would beset the scholars of the future as to the existence of two thinkers, who, both Englishmen, both bearing the name of Bacon, agreed in assigning an important place in their doctrines to empirical knowledge? M. Pais has dismissed a great many ancient Roman traditions as mere legend, for almost no other reason than that the same names, associated with tolerably similar episodes, are in a like manner seen to repeat themselves. With all due respect to the criticism of plagiarism, whose spirit denies the spontaneous repetition of events or words, coincidence is one of those freaks which cannot be eliminated from history.

But it cannot be enough simply to acknowledge the broad possibility of coincidence. Reduced to this simple statement, criticism would waver eternally between pro and con. For doubt to become the tool of knowledge it is necessary, in each particular case, that the degree of probability of coincidence can be weighed with some exactitude. Here the path of historical research, like that of so many other disciplines of the mind, intersects the royal highway of the theory of probabilities.

To evaluate the probability of an event is to weigh its chances of taking place. That granted, is it legitimate to speak of the possibility of a past event? Obviously not, in the absolute sense. Only the future has contingency. The past is something already given which leaves no room for possibility. Before the die was cast, the probability that any number might appear was one to six. The problem vanishes as soon as the dice box is emptied. Somewhat later we may not be sure whether, upon that day, a three or a five actually turned up. The uncertainty, then, exists in us, in our memory, or in that of our witnesses, and not in the things themselves.

In a correct analysis, however, the use which historical research makes of the idea of probabilities is not at all contradictory. When the historian asks himself about the probability of a past event, he actually attempts to transport himself, by a bold exercise of the mind, to the time before the event itself, in order to gauge its chances, as they appeared upon the eve of its realization. Hence, probability remains properly in the future. But since the line of the present has somehow been moved back in the imagination, it is a future of bygone times built upon a fragment which, for us, is actually the past. If it is incontestible that the event has taken place, these speculations have little more value than that of a metaphysical game. What was the probability that Napoleon would be born? That Adolf Hitler, the soldier of 1914, would escape French bullets? We are not forbidden to amuse ourselves with these questions, providing we understand them for what they really are: simple rhetorical devices intended to illuminate the role of contingency and of the unforeseeable in the progress of mankind. They have nothing to do with the criticism of evidence. It is otherwise when the very existence of the fact seems uncertain. For example, are we in doubt whether an author could spontaneously have repeated many of the episodes, even many of the words, of another narrative, without having copied it? Can we believe that chance alone, or some divinely preordained harmony, suffices to explain the very striking resemblance between *The Protocols of the Wise Men of Zion* and the pamphlet of an obscure polemicist of the Second Empire? According as such a coincidence should appear to have a greater or lesser coefficient of probability prior to the composition of the narrative, we shall either acknowledge or reject its likelihood today.

For all that, the mathematics of chance are based upon a fiction. From the outset, they postulate impartial conditions in all possible cases: a specific cause favoring a certain outcome in advance would be like a foreign body in the calculation. The die of the theoretician is a perfectly balanced cube; were a single grain of lead to be slipped under one of its surfaces, the chances of the players would cease to be equal. But, in the criticism of evidence, almost all the dice are loaded. For extremely delicate human elements constantly intervene to tip the balance toward a preferred possibility.

One historical discipline, strictly speaking, is excepted. It is linguistics, or, at least, that branch of it which is concerned with establishing the relationships between languages. It is very different from critical studies in the strict sense, yet it shares with these studies the common characteristic of seeking to discover affiliations. Now, the terms upon which it reasons are extraordinary close to the *a priori* convention of equality, as found in the theory of chance. It owes this prerogative to the very peculiarities of linguistic phenomena. Indeed, not only does the immense number of possible combinations of sounds reduce to virtual insignificance the probability of any considerable fortuitous repetition in different languages but, what is still more important, the meanings attributed to these combinations are entirely arbitrary, aside from some few imitative onomatopœic words. No association of prior ideas dictates that the sound of *tu,* as it is pronounced in either French or Latin, should serve to indicate the second person. If, then, we find that this sound has this role in French, in Italian, in Spanish, and in Rumanian—if we simultaneously observe a mass of other equally irrational similarities between these languages—the only sensible explanation would be that French, Italian, Spanish, and Rumanian have a common origin. Because the various possibilities were unaffected by human interests, a practically pure mathematical calculation of the chances has carried the decision.

But this simplicity is far from the norm.

Several of the charters of a medieval sovereign, dealing with different matters, repeat the same words and the same constructions. Therefore, the fanatics of "stylistic criticism" assert that they were drawn up by the same notary. This might be granted, were chance the sole consideration. But such is not the case. Each society and, still more, each little professional group has its habits of language. As a result, it is not enough to enumerate the points of similarity. It is further necessary to distinguish the unusual from the commonplace among them. Only the really exceptional expression can identify an author; assuming, of course, that its repetitions are sufficiently numerous. The error here lies in attributing equal weight to all elements of speech: whereas in fact the variable coefficients of social preference affecting each of them are like the grains of lead which upset the equality of chance.

Since the beginning of the nineteenth century, a whole school of learned men has devoted itself to the study of the transmission of literary texts. The principle is simple. We have three manuscripts of the same work: B, C, and D. We may ascertain that all three give the same, obviously erroneous, reading. (This is the method of errors, the oldest method, that of Lachmann.) Or, more often, we find that all three show the same readings, whether good or bad, but different from most of those of other manuscripts. (This is the complete listing of the variants recommended by Don Quentin.) In either case, we should decide that the three are "related." Depending upon the circumstances, it would be understood either that they had been copied from each other in a sequence which remains to be determined, or that they all derived by separate ancestries from a common model. In short, it is quite certain that such a sustained coincidence could not be fortuitous. Nevertheless, two observations of rather recent date have forced textual criticism to abandon much of the quasimechanical rigor of its first conclusions.

Copyists have sometimes corrected their model. Even when they worked independently from each other, common mental habits must very often have suggested similar conclusions. Terence somewhere uses the word *raptio*, which is extremely rare. Not understanding it, two scribes substituted *ratio*, which makes no sense but which was familiar to them. In so doing, was it necessary for them to act either in concert or in imitation of each other? There you see one type of error which is practically incapable of teaching us anything about the "genealogy" of manuscripts. There is more. Why should the copyist use only a single model? When he was able to compare several copies, he was not forbidden ultimately to choose from among the variants to the best of his ability. Certainly, this was very seldom the case in the Middle Ages, when libraries were scanty; to all appearance, it was much more frequent in antiquity. What place are we to assign to those incestuous fruits of several different traditions upon the beautiful trees of Jephthah which are customarily drawn up at the beginning of critical editions? The will of the individual, like the pressure of collective forces, cheats pure chance in the game of coincidences.

Thus, as the philosophy of the eighteenth century had already seen with Volney, the majority of the problems of historical criticism are really problems of probability, but such that the subtlest calculation must own itself incapable of their solution. It is not only that its data are extraordinarily complex. Most frequently, by their very nature they are unamenable to any mathematical translation. For example, how are we to calculate the particular preference which a society accords to a word or a custom? The science of a Fermat, a Laplace, and an Émile Borel will not rid us of our difficulties. But at least, since it is placed at the inaccessible extremity of our logic, we may call upon it to aid us, from on high, toward a better analysis of our reasoning.

He who has not lived among scholars does not realize how loath they ordinarily are to admit the innocence of a coincidence. Because two similar expressions are found in both the Salic law and an edict of Clovis, a reputable German savant has declared that the law must have derived from that prince. Let us pass over the banality of words used here and there. A mere tinge of mathematical theory would be enough to prevent such a false idea. When chance has a free hand, the order of probability of a single coincidence or of a small number of coincidences is seldom impossibly high. Even if they seem astonishing to us, the surprises of common sense are rarely sensations of much value.

It may be amusing to calculate the probability that a stroke of chance should fix the deaths of two entirely separate personages upon the same day of the same month of two different years. It is equal to $1/365^2$.[3]

---

[3] This would be correct on the supposition that the chances of dying were equal for each day of the year. This is not exact (there is an annual curve of mortality), but it may be conveniently postulated here.

Let us now grant (despite the absurdity of the postulate) that the suppression of the orders of both John Colombini and Ignatius Loyola by the Roman Church was preordained. The examination of the pontifical lists enables us to establish that the probability of the abolition by two popes of the same name was as 11 to 13. The combined probability of the deaths falling on the same day of the same month and of two homonymous popes being the authors of the condemnation falls somewhere between 1/1,000 and 1/1,000,000.[4] Doubtless, no betting man would be satisfied with these odds. But the natural sciences consider as next to impracticable, on the earthly scale, even possibili-

---

[4] From the death of John Colombini until today, 65 popes have ruled the church (including the dual and triple papacies of the period of the Great Schism); since the death of Ignatius there have been 38. The first list gives 55 who are homonymous with the second, in which these same names are repeated exactly 38 times (the popes, as we know, customarily taking names already hallowed by tradition.)

The probability that the Jesuates would be suppressed by one of these homonymous popes was, therefore 55/65 or 11/13. For the Jesuits, it rose to 38/38 or 1; in other words, it became a certainty. The combined probability is of 11/13 times 1, or 11/13. Finally, $1/365^2$ or 1/133,225 times 11/13 equals 11/1,731,925, which is equal to slightly more than 1/157,447. To be entirely accurate, it would be necessary to take into account the respective durations of the pontificates. But the nature of this mathematical diversion, whose sole object is to shed light upon the order of magnitude, appeared to me to justify simplification of the calculations.

[*Translator's note: The reader should here recall that Marc Bloch's manuscript was incomplete, and that, during the writing of it, he had no access to those reference books with which he would certainly have checked and corrected the mathematical inaccuracies contained in this passage. In any case, these inaccuracies do not affect the main line of the reasoning, which is essentially correct.*]

ties of the order of 10/15. Obviously, we are wide of the mark—with good reason, as the reliably verified example of the two saints bears witness. It is in the accumulation of coincidences that the probability becomes practically negligible: for, by virtue of a well-known theorem, the probabilities of simple facts must be multiplied by each other in order to give the probability of the combination, and, since the probabilities are fractions their product is, by definition, smaller than its components. In linguistics, there is the famous example of the word *bad,* which means the same thing in English and Persian, although the term has not the faintest common origin in the two languages. Anyone who should pretend to found a connection upon this isolated agreement would sin against the main law of all criticism of coincidences: "Only large numbers are conclusive."

The substantial agreements or disagreements are composed of a multitude of specific circumstances. All things considered, accidental influences cancel each other out. If, on the other hand, we should consider each element separately from the others, the effect of these variables can no longer be eliminated. Even if the dice have been loaded, an isolated throw will always be more difficult to foresee than the outcome of the game; consequently, once played, it will be subject to a much greater variety of explanations. That is why the further criticism delves into detail the more its probabilities tend to be blurred. Taken separately, there is scarcely a word in our modern version of

Oresteia which we may be certain of reading as Æschylus wrote it. In its entirety, however, we need have no misgivings that our *Oresteia* is really that of Æschylus. There is more certainty in the whole than in its parts.

To what extent, however, are we justified in mouthing this glorious word "certainty"? Mabillon, long ago, admitted that the criticism of charters could not attain "metaphysical" certainty. He was quite right. It is only for the sake of simplification that we sometimes speak of evidence rather than of probabilities. But we are more aware today than in Mabillon's time, that that convention is not peculiar to us. It is not "impossible," in the absolute sense of the term, that the *Donation of Constantine* is authentic, or—according to the whim of some scholars—that the *Germania* of Tacitus is a forgery. Nor is it, in the same sense, "impossible" that a monkey might accidentally reconstruct either the *Donation* or the *Germania,* letter for letter, simply by striking the keys of a typewriter at random. "The impossible physical event," Cournot has said, "is nothing but an event whose probability is infinitely small." So far as it finds certainty only by estimating the probable and the improbable, historical criticism is like most other sciences of reality, except that it undoubtedly deals with a more subtle gradation of degrees.

Do we always rightly appreciate the immense advance embodied in the advent of a rational method of criticism applied to human testimony? Advance, I mean, not only for historical knowledge but for knowledge as a whole.

Not long ago, unless there were very good reasons, in advance, for suspecting witnesses or narrators of falsehood, three fourths of all facts stated were facts accepted. Nor was it very long ago. Lucien Febvre has excellently demonstrated, for the Renaissance, that men neither thought nor acted differently then than in periods quite close to ours, which is why their masterpieces are still a living inspiration for us. Nor should we say that such was, by nature, the attitude of that credulous throng whose ponderous mass—misled, alas! by more than one pseudo-savant—is constantly threatening even in our own day to sweep our fragile civilizations into the abyss of ignorance and folly. The steadiest minds did not and could not escape the common prejudices at the time. Was it told that a shower of blood had fallen? Why, then, there are showers of blood. If Montaigne read in his beloved ancients this or that nonsense about a land whose people were born without heads or about the miraculous strength of the little fish known as the remora, he set them down among his serious arguments without raising an eyebrow. For all his ingenuity in dismantling the machinery of a false rumor, he was far more suspicious of prevailing ideas than of so-called attested facts. In this way, as in the Rabelaisian myth, old man Hearsay ruled over the physical as well as the human world. Perhaps even more over the physical world than the human. For, having a more direct experience, men sooner doubted a human event than a meteor or an alleged irregularity of organic life. If your philosophy was repelled by miracles, or your religion by the miracles of other religions, you had to force yourself painfully to find in these strange manifestations some ostensibly intelligible causes. Whether works of the devil, or occult influences, these "causes" still belonged to a system of ideas or images completely foreign to what we should today call scientific thought. The audacity of denying the manifestations themselves scarcely entered anyone's head. Pompanozzi, shining star of that Paduan school so opposed to Christian supernaturalism, did not believe that kings, *simply because they were kings* even if anointed with oil from the sacred ampulla, could cure sick persons by touching them with their hands. Nevertheless, he did not dispute the cures. He explained them by a physiological peculiarity which he conceived as hereditary: the glorious privilege of a sacred function was reduced to the curative virtue of a dynastic spittle.

Now, if today we have been able to clear our picture of the universe of so many fictitious marvels, seemingly confirmed by the agreement of generations, we are doubtless primarily indebted to the gradual evolution of the idea of a natural order governed by immutable laws. But this notion itself could not have been established so solidly, the observations which seemed to contradict it could not have been eliminated, except by the patient labor of an experiment performed upon man himself as a witness. We are enabled henceforth both to expose and to explain the imperfections of evidence. We have acquired the right of disbelief, because we understand, better than in the past, when and why we ought to disbelieve. And it is by this means that science has succeeded in throwing off the dead weight of a great many spurious problems.

But, here as elsewhere, pure knowledge is not divorced from action.

Richard Simon, whose name stands among the first rank of our founding fathers, has not merely left us some admirable lessons in exegesis. He also used his keen mind to rescue simple souls persecuted by the stupid accusation of witchcraft. There is nothing arbitrary in the coincidence. In both roles, the need for intellectual discipline is the same. The same instrument served both needs. Obliged always to be guided by the reports of others, legal action is no less interested than pure research in weighing their accuracy. The tools at its disposal are not different from those of scholarship. They are in fact those which scholarship originally forged. In the useful employment of doubt, judicial practice has only followed, rather laggingly, in the footsteps of the Bollandists and the Benedictines. And the psychologists themselves did not think to seek a scientific object in human testimony, as directly observed and elicited, until long after the confused memory of the past had begun to be subjected to a rational proof. It is a scandal that in our own age, which is more than ever exposed to the poisons of fraud and false rumor, the critical method is so completely absent from our school programs. It has ceased to be the mere humble auxiliary to exercises of the study. Henceforth, far wider horizons open before it, and history may reckon among its most certain glories that, by this elaboration of its technique, it has pioneered for mankind a new path to truth and, hence, to justice.

CHAPTER IV

HISTORICAL ANALYSIS

1. *Judging or Understanding?*

THE FORMULA of the venerable Ranke is famous: the historian has no other aim than to describe things "as they happened, *wie es eigentlich gewesen.*" Herodotus had earlier expressed it: "to narrate what was, *ton eonta.*" In other words, the scholar, the historian, is urged to efface himself before the facts. Perhaps, like many maxims, this one has owed its success only to its ambiguity. We can plainly read in it a counsel of integrity: this, we cannot doubt, was Ranke's meaning. But there was, besides, a counsel of passivity, so that we here see two problems arising simultaneously: that of historical impartiality, and that of history as an attempt at reproduction or as an attempt at analysis.

But if there is really a problem of impartiality, it derives solely from the fact that the word is itself equivocal.

There are two ways of being impartial: that of the scholar and that of the judge. They have a common root in their honest submission to the truth. The scholar records—better still, he invites—the experience which may, perhaps, upset his most cherished theories.

The good judge, whatever his secret heart's desire, questions witnesses with no other concern than to know the facts, whatever they may be. For both this is an obligation of conscience which is never questioned.

However, there comes a moment when their paths divide. When the scholar has observed and explained, his task is finished. It yet remains for the judge to pass sentence. If, imposing silence on his personal inclination, he pronounces it according to the law, he will be deemed impartial. And he will be impartial in a judicial sense, not in a scientific sense. For we can neither condemn nor absolve without accepting a table of values which no longer refers to any positive science. That one man has killed another is a fact which is eminently susceptible of proof. But to punish the murderer assumes that we consider murder culpable: which is, after all, only an opinion about which not all civilizations have agreed.

Now, for a long time, the historian has passed for a sort of judge in Hades, charged with meting out praise or blame to dead heroes. We cannot but believe that this attitude satisfies a deep-rooted instinct. For all teachers who have had to correct their students' papers know how reluctantly these youngsters are dissuaded from playing the role of Minos or Osiris from behind their desks. The words of Pascal are more to the point than ever: "We all play God in judging: this is good or this is evil." Men forget that a value judgment has a *raison d'être* only as preparation for an action and a meaning solely in relation to a system of consciously accepted moral references. In daily life, the demands of conduct compel us to use these ordinarily rather summary labels. Where we can no longer act, where commonly accepted ideas differ profoundly from our own, such labels become an embarrassment. Are we so sure of ourselves and of our age as to divide the company of our forefathers into the just and the damned? How absurd it is, by elevating the entirely relative criteria of one individual, one party, or one generation to the absolute, to inflict standards upon the way in which Sulla governed Rome, or Richelieu the States of the Most Christian King! Moreover, since nothing is more variable than such judgments, subject to all the fluctuations of collective opinion or personal caprice, history, by all too frequently preferring the compilation of honor rolls to that of notebooks, has gratuitously given itself the appearance of the most uncertain of disciplines. Hollow indictments are followed by vain rehabilitations. Robespierrists! Anti-Robespierrists! For pity's sake, simply tell us what Robespierre was.

If the judgment only followed the explanation, the reader could simply skip it. Unfortunately the habit of passing judgments leads to a loss of taste for explanations. When the passions of the past blend with the prejudices of the present, human reality is reduced to a picture in black and white. Montaigne has already warned us on this head: "Whenever judgment leans to one side we cannot help distorting and twisting the narrative in this direction." Moreover, to plumb the consciousness of another person, separated from us by the interval of generations, we must virtually lay aside our own ego, whereas, to say what we think, we need only remain ourselves. This is a less arduous endeavor. How much easier it is to write for or against Luther than to fathom his soul; to believe Pope Gregory VII about Emperor Henry IV, or Henry IV about Gregory VII, than to unravel the underlying causes of one of the greatest dramas of Western civilization!

To rise above questions of personality, consider the problem of the land confiscated during the Revolution. During the Terror, and reversing the earlier legislation, the government decided to sell it off in small lots without competitive bidding. Unquestionably, this seriously compromised the best interests of the Treasury. Certain modern scholars have burst out angrily against this policy. What courage they would have displayed, had they dared to say so while sitting in the Convention! Far from the guillotine, this violence without danger may amuse us, but it would be more worthwhile to investigate what it was that the men of the Year III really wanted. Primarily, they hoped to favor the acquisition of the land by the little people of the rural area; in preference to the balancing of the budget, they sought the relief of the poor peasants, as a guarantee of their fidelity to the new order. Were they right or wrong? What do I care for a historian's belated decision on this point? We should only beg him not to be so hypnotized by his own choice as to forget that at the time another was possible. Nevertheless, the lesson of the intellectual development of mankind is clear: the sciences have shown themselves ever more fruitful and, hence, in the long run more practical, in proportion as they deliberately abandon the old anthropocentrism of good and evil. Today, we should laugh at a chemist who separated the bad gases, like chlorine, from the good ones like oxygen. But, had chemistry adopted this classification in its infancy, it would have run the grave risk of getting stuck there, to the great detriment of the knowledge of matter.

However, let us beware of pushing the analogy too far. The nomenclature of the science of man will always have its peculiar characteristics. That of the science of the physical world excludes teleological doctrine. There the words "success" or "failure," "incompetence" or "ability" could, at best, play the role only of fictions, forever laden with dangers. On the other hand, they belong to the normal vocabulary of history. For history has to do with beings who are, by nature, capable of pursuing conscious ends.

We may admit that an army commander who is engaged in a battle usually strives to win it. If the forces are approximately equal on either side, and he loses, it is perfectly legitimate to say that he has maneuvered poorly. If such mishaps were habitual with him, we should not deviate from the most scrupulous judgment of fact by observing that he was, doubtless, not a very good strategist. Again, if we are considering a monetary alteration, whose aim, let us assume, was to favor debtors at the expense of creditors, to term it either excellent or deplorable would be to take sides with one of the two groups, and thereby arbitrarily to transfer into the past an entirely subjective idea of public welfare. But let us imagine that, by some chance, the operation intended to lighten the burden of debt has ended in actual fact—such cases are known—in the contrary result. "It failed," we say, without thereby doing anything more than honestly stating a reality. As in psychology as a whole, the unsuccessful act is one of the essential data of human evolution.

There is something else. Has our general, perchance, led his troops to defeat intentionally? We should not hesitate to charge him with treason: because in plain language that is the proper word for it. It would be a pedantic refinement for history to reject the aid of the simple and direct vocabulary of common usage. Next, we must still try to understand how common contemporary ethics regarded such an act. Treason can be a sort of conformity, as with the condottieri of bygone Italy.

When all is said and done, a single word, "understanding," is the beacon light of our studies. Let us not say that the true historian is a stranger to emotion: he has that, at all events. "Understanding," in all honesty, is a word pregnant with difficulties, but also with hope. Moreover, it is a friendly word. Even in action, we are far too prone to judge. It is so easy to denounce. We are never sufficiently understanding. Whoever differs from us—a foreigner or a political adversary—is almost inevitably considered evil. A little more understanding of people would be necessary merely for guidance, in the conflicts which are unavoidable; all the more to prevent them while there is yet time. If history would only renounce its false archangelic airs, it would help us to cure this weakness. It includes a vast experience of human diversities, a continuous contact with men. Life, like science, has everything to gain from it, if only these contacts be friendly.

2. From the Diversity of Human Functions to the Unity of Consciences

Understanding, however, has nothing of the attitude of passivity about it. Two things will always be necessary for the practice of a science: a subject-matter, but also a man. Human reality, like that of the physical world, is vast and variegated. A mere photograph, even supposing that such a mechanically complete reproduction had meaning, would be undecipherable. Is it suggested that the documents have already inserted a preliminary screen between past and present? Certainly, they often eliminate at random. On the other hand, they almost never organize their subject-matter according to the demands of an intelligence which seeks to know. Like any scholar, like any mind which perceives at all, the historian selects and sorts. In short, he analyzes. And, to begin with, he seeks out the similarities in order to compare them.

. . .

I have before me a Roman funerary inscription, carved from a single block, made for a single purpose. Yet nothing could be more variegated than the evidences which there await the probing of the scholar's lancet.

If we are especially interested in linguistic matters, the words and the syntax express the state of Latin as men sought to write it in that time and place, and through the transparency of its half-erudite language we may be able to catch a glimpse of everyday speech. On the other hand, should our predilection incline towards the study of beliefs, we are at the very core of otherworldly aspirations. Or, if toward the political system, we are overjoyed at the name of an emperor or the date of a magistracy. Toward the economy, the epitaph may perhaps reveal an unknown trade. And I pass over the other possibilities. Instead of an isolated document, let us now consider any given moment in the evolution of a civilization which is known through a number and variety of documents. There was not one of the men then alive who did not participate almost at one and the same time in multiple manifestations of human activity; who did not speak to and make himself understood by his neighbors; who did not have his gods; who was not a producer, trader, or merely a consumer; who, if he took no part in political events, did not at least experience their consequences. Should we venture to recount all these activities without selection and rearrangement, in the very same confusion in which each document, each individual or collective life presents them to us? That would be to sacrifice clarity, not to the true order of reality—which is composed of natural affinities and underlying connections—but to the purely superficial order of contemporaneousness. A notebook of experiments is not to be confused with the moment-by-moment diary of everything that has happened in the laboratory.

For when we think we see a kinship between certain phenomena in the course of human evolution, what is it we mean except that each type of institution, belief, practice, or event thus classified appears to us to express a particular and, up to a certain point, a permanent tendency of the individual or society? For example, should we deny that, despite all contrasts, all religious emotions have something in common? It necessarily follows that we shall always better understand any human fact if we already have an understanding of other facts of the same sort. The use of money in the first period of feudalism, more as a standard of values than as a means of payment, differed profoundly from the established norms of Western economy about 1850; in turn there is scarcely less contrast between the monetary systems of the mid-nineteenth century and that of today. However, I submit that a scholar who knew only the currency of about the year 1000 would find it difficult to grasp the peculiarities of its use even at that date. It is this which justifies certain specializations which are, in a sense, vertical: justifies them in the limited way in which specializations can be justified; that is, as correctives to the lack of breadth of our minds, and the short span of our lives.

To neglect to organize rationally what comes to us as raw material is in the long run only to deny time—hence, history itself. For can we understand this or that period of Latin if we detach it from the earlier development of the language? This form of ownership, or those beliefs were not, of course, absolute beginnings. Inasmuch as their development proceeds from the most ancient to the most recent times, human phenomena are governed primarily by chains of similar phenomena. To classify them according to kind is to lay bare the principal effective lines of force.

But, some will object, the distinctions which you establish in this way by cutting across life itself exist only in your mind; they do not exist in reality, where everything is intermingled. Moreover, you are making use of "abstraction." Granted. But why be afraid of words? No science could dispense with "abstractions" any more than it could dispense with imagination. Be it said in passing, it is significant that the same thinkers who would banish the former generally display an equal ill-humor towards the latter. It is the same badly understood positivism in both cases. The sciences of man are no exception. In what way is the function of chlorophyll more "real," in the absolute sense, than the economic function? Only those classifications which depend upon false resemblances would be disastrous. It is the business of the historian to be always testing his classifications in order to justify their existence and, if it seems advisable, to revise them. Moreover, despite their common effort to encompass reality, they may start from very different vantage points.

For example, we have "the history of law." The textbooks, always admirable tools of sclerosis, have popularized the term. But, what does it mean? A legal rule is a social norm, explicitly imperative, sanctioned by an authority capable of imposing respect by an exact system of compulsions and penalties. In practice, such precepts can govern the most diversified activities. They are never the sole means of controlling them: in our daily conduct, we are constantly complying with moral, professional, or fashionable codes which often make different demands from those of the code of the law. Moreover, the frontiers of the latter are constantly fluctuating; and, obviously, a socially recognized obligation does not change its nature simply by being inserted in the law, even if it can acquire more or less force or clarity thereby. Hence, law, in the strict sense of the word, is only the formal covering of realities which are in themselves too diversified to furnish profitable subject-matter for a single study. Moreover, it exhausts none of these realities. Take the family—whether it be a question of the small matrimonial family of today in a state of perpetual expansion and contraction or of the great medieval house, that community consolidated by such a lasting network of feelings and interests—for a true insight into its life, would it ever be sufficient simply to enumerate, one after the other, the articles of any family law? Some men seem to think so—how grievously they were deceived is sufficiently demonstrated by our inability to retrace the inward evolution of the French family even today.

However, there is certainly something very real in the notion of juridical fact as distinct from others. This is because, in many societies at least, the application, and even in great measure the elaboration, of rules of law have been the particular work of a group of relatively specialized men. This group, whose members could of course combine their legal role with other social functions, has been sufficiently autonomous to have its own traditions and often even the practice of a particular method of reasoning. In short, it may be that the history of law has no separate existence except as the history of jurists; but this is not a bad sort of existence for a branch of the sciences of man. Understood in this sense, the history of law sheds some glimmers of light upon phenomena which are extremely diversified, yet subject to a common human activity, and these glimmerings, if necessarily limited in their scope, are very revealing.

A different kind of subject is represented by what we usually call "human geography." Here the angle of sight does not come from a professional mentality, as is the case, however unsuspected, with the history of law. Nor does it, like religious or economic history, arise from the specific nature of a human fact, either of the beliefs, emotions, outpourings of the heart, hopes and fears inspired by the vision of forces transcending humanity, or of the efforts to satisfy and organize material needs. The inquiry is focused upon a type of connection common to a great number of social phenomena. "Anthropo-geography" studies societies in their relations to their physical environments: relations which are obviously mutual, since man is constantly acting upon things at the same time that they are acting upon him. In this case again, therefore, we have nothing more nor less than a perspective whose legitimacy is proved by its fruitfulness, but which must be supplemented by other perspectives to be complete. Such, indeed, is the true function of analysis in any category of research. Science dissects reality only in order to observe it better by virtue of a play of converging searchlights whose beams continually intermingle and interpenetrate each other. Danger threatens only when each searchlight operator claims to see everything by himself, when each canton of learning pretends to national sovereignty.

Once more, however, we must beware of postulating any false geometric parallels between the sciences of nature and a science of man. From the view which I have from my window, each savant selects his proper subject without troubling himself too much about the whole. The physicist explains the blue of the sky; the chemist the water of the brook; the botanist the plants. The task of reassembling the landscape as it appears to me and excites my imagination, they leave to art, should any painter or poet wish to undertake it. The fact is that the landscape as a unity exists only in my consciousness. Now, the peculiarity of the scientific method, as practiced and justified by the success of these branches of learning, is that it deliberately abandons the observer in order to know more about the thing observed. To the natural sciences, the connections which our mind weaves between things appear arbitrary; they deliberately break them in order to re-establish a diversity which seems to them more authentic. Even so, however, the organic world poses singularly delicate problems. For greater convenience, the biologist may indeed study respiration, digestion, or the motor functions separately; for all that, he is not unaware that there is a whole person for which he must account. The difficulties of history are of still another nature. For in the last analysis it is human consciousness which is the subject-matter of history. The interrelations, confusions, and infections of human consciousness are, for history, reality itself.

As for *homo religiosus, homo œconomicus, homo politicus,* and all that rigmarole of Latinized men, the list of which we could string out indefinitely, there is grave danger of mistaking them for something else than they really are: phantoms which are convenient providing they do not become nuisances. The man of flesh and bone, reuniting them all simultaneously, is the only real being.

Certainly, our minds have interior partitions which some have been peculiarly adept at raising. Gustave Lenôtre was constantly amazed to find so many excellent fathers of families among the Terrorists. Even if our great revolutionaries had actually been the bloodthirsty monsters whose portraits so agreeably titillate a middle-class public, such amazement would none the less betray a rather limited psychology. How many men lead lives on three or four different levels, which they wish and sometimes succeed in keeping apart?

However, this is far from denying the deep-seated unity of the ego and the constant intermingling of its various attitudes. Were Pascal, the mathematician, and Pascal, the Christian, strangers to each other? Did François Rabelais, the learned physician, and Master Alcofribas of Pantagruelist memory, never cross paths? Even though the roles played alternately by the same actor seem to conflict as crudely as the stereotyped characters of a melodrama, it may be that this antithesis, correctly considered, is only the mask of a deeper solidarity. Men poked fun at the elegiac Florian, who, it appears, beat his mistresses. Perhaps he lavished so much sweetness in his verses to console himself for his failure to employ more of it in his conduct. When the medieval merchant, after spending the day in violating church commandments on usury and just prices, went off to kneel sanctimoniously before the image of Our Lady, or when in the evening of his life he heaped up pious charitable endowments; when the great manufacturer of a sterner age built hospitals with money saved out of the wages of ragged children, were either of them seeking, as is usually said, only to obtain a rather cheap insurance against heavenly wrath, or were they not rather, by these outbursts of faith or philanthropy, also satisfying, almost without conscious recognition, those secret needs of the heart which harsh daily routine had forced them to repress? There are contradictions which closely resemble evasions.

Let us pass from the individual to society. To say that the latter is simply the sum of individual minds would be to say too little, but, all things considered, it is at least their product; and we should not, therefore, be surprised to discover the same play of continuous interaction. It is an established fact that from the twelfth century until at least the Reformation the communities of textile workers were one of the favorite breeding-grounds of heresies. That is surely a worthwhile matter for a note on religious history. Let us then file this little card carefully in its drawer. And let us throw some more notes into the neighboring pigeonhole, the one marked "economic history." Are we to believe that, by this means, we have finished with these heretical weavers? We have still to explain them, since one of their fundamental characteristics was not merely that they made their religious and economic lives coexist, but that they blended them together. Lucien Febvre is impressed by the "certainty, or security, of moral tone" which the several generations just prior to our own apparently enjoyed so fully. He finds two principal reasons for it: the dominance over men's minds of the cosmological system of Laplace, and the "abnormal stability" of money. No two human facts are apparently more unlike. Nevertheless, they worked together to give a society its characteristic mental attitude.

Certainly such relationships are just as complex on the collective scale as in the individual mind. Today we should no longer dare to say without qualification that literature is "the expression of society." That is by no means true—at least not in the sense that a mirror is the "expression" of the object which it reflects. Literature may as easily express a defense reaction to its society as an acceptance of it. Almost inevitably, it carries along a great number of inherited themes, of formal devices learned in the study, of outworn æsthetic conventions, which act as so many causes of retardation. As H. Focillon sagely observes: "At any given date, the political, the economic and the artistic do not occupy [I should have preferred "do not necessarily occupy"] the same position on their respective curves." Because of these disparities social life maintains a rhythm which is nearly always uneven. In the same way, with the majority of individuals, the various psyches, to speak the pluralist language of old-fashioned psychology, are seldom of an identical age. How many mature men still preserve streaks of childishness!

In 1837, Michelet explained to Sainte-Beuve: "If I had introduced only political history into my narrative, if I had taken no account of the diverse elements of history (religion, law, geography, literature, art, etc.), my procedure would have been quite different. *But a great vital movement was needed, because all these diverse elements gravitated together in the unity of the story.*" A generation later, Fustel de Coulanges, in his turn, announced to his listeners in the Sorbonne:

"Supposing a hundred specialists had divided the past of France according to lot, do you think that, in the end, they would have written the history of France? I very much doubt it. At the very least, they should miss the linkage of facts: *now, this linkage is itself a historical truth.*" The contrast of the images is significant. Michelet thought and felt in terms of the organic; Fustel, son of an age for which the Newtonian universe seemed to furnish the ultimate scientific pattern, took his metaphors from space. Their fundamental agreement is all the more impressive. These two great historians were too great to overlook the fact that a civilization, like a person, is no mechanically arranged game of solitaire; the knowledge of fragments, studied by turns, each for its own sake, will never produce the knowledge of the whole; it will not even produce that of the fragments themselves.

But the work of reintegration can come only after analysis. Better still, it is only the continuation of analysis, and its ultimate justification. In the scene as we first perceive it, which we contemplate rather than observe, and in which therefore nothing is distinct, we cannot discern the interrelationships. Their delicate network becomes visible only after the elements have been classified. Moreover, in order to remain true to life in its intertwining actions and reactions, we need not pretend to seize it as a whole. Such an attempt is too vast for the powers of a single scholar. Nothing is more legitimate, nothing is more salutary than to center the study of a society upon one of its particular aspects, or, better still, upon one of the well-defined problems underlying one or another of these aspects: the beliefs, the economy, the class or group structure, the political crises. . . .

By this systematic selection, not only will the problems usually be more concretely stated, but even the facts of connection and interchange will stand out with greater clarity. Provided only that we want to discover them. Do you expect really to know the great merchants of Renaissance Europe, vendors of cloth or spices, monopolists in copper, mercury, or alum, bankers of kings and the Emperor, by knowing their merchandise alone? Bear in mind that they were painted by Holbein, that they read Erasmus or Luther. To understand the attitude of the medieval vassal to his seigneur you must inform yourself about his attitude toward his God as well. The historian never escapes from time. But, in an inevitable oscillation, already treated above in the discussion of origins, he sometimes considers the great waves of related phenomena which run over long periods, and sometimes the specific moments in which these currents are channeled into the powerful vortex of direct experience.

3. *Nomenclature*

Nevertheless, it would be trivial to confine ourselves to distinguishing the main aspects of the activities of either a person or a society. Within each of these broad groups of facts, a new and more delicate effort to analysis is necessary. We must distinguish the various institutions which compose a political system, the various beliefs, practices, and emotions which make up a religion. Within these fragments and in the whole itself, we must characterize those features in which they resemble, or in which they differ from, other realities of the same category . . . all problems of classification which are inseparable, in practice, from the fundamental problem of nomenclature.

For the first tool needed by any analysis is an appropriate language; a language capable of describing the precise outlines of the facts, while preserving the necessary flexibility to adapt itself to further discoveries and, above all, a language which is neither vacillating nor ambiguous. Now, there is where the shoe pinches us historians. One keen-minded writer with no particular love for us has seen this clearly: "The great day of definitions, of distinct and special terms, to replace those of confused or merely statistical origin, has not yet arrived for history." So declares M. Paul Valéry. But if this day of precision has not yet arrived, is it not possible that it may yet come? And why, to begin with, is it so slow in coming?

Chemistry has fashioned its own supply of symbols, and even its own words. "Gas," if I am not mistaken, is one of the few genuinely invented words belonging to the French language. That is because chemistry had the great advantage of being applied to realities which were, by their very nature, incapable of naming themselves. The language of confused perception which it has rejected is no less removed from its objects and, in this sense, no less arbitrary than that of the classified and controlled observation which it has substituted for it: whether we call it vitriol or sulfuric acid, the substance itself has not influenced the choice. It is quite otherwise with a science of humanity. Men gave names to their actions, their beliefs, and the various aspects of their social life without waiting until they became objects of disinterested research. Hence, history receives its vocubulary, for the most part, from the very subject-matter of its study. It accepts it, already worn out and deformed by long usage; frequently, moreover, ambiguous from the very beginning, like any system of expression which has not derived from the rigorously organized efforts of technical experts.

The worst is that these borrowings themselves lack unity. The documents tend to impose their own nomenclature; if he harkens to them, the historian is taking dictation from an epoch which is each time different. But of course he is thinking according to the categories of his own time, consequently with its words. Should we speak of patricians, a contemporary of the venerable Cato would understand us. On the other hand, should an author speak of the role of "the bourgeoisie" in the crises of the Roman Empire, how would he translate either the word or the idea into Latin? Thus, two distinct orientations almost necessarily divide the language of history. Let us examine each in its turn.

• • •

To reproduce or copy the terminology of the past might, at first sight, seem a rather safe course. In application, however, it would encounter manifold difficulties. In the first place, changes in things do not by any means always entail similar changes in their names. Such is the natural consequence of the traditionalist character of all language, and of the lack of inventiveness common to most men.

The observation is valid even for utilitarian appliances, despite the fact that these are ordinarily subject to rather clearcut changes in form and construction. If my neighbor tells me that he is going out in his coupé, or his limousine, am I to understand that he is referring to a horse-drawn carriage, or to an automobile? Only my prior knowledge of his coach-house or his garage will enable me to answer. As a rule, *aratrum* meant a plow without wheels; *carruca,* a plow with wheels. However, since the first appeared before the second, can I be certain, if I find the old word in a text, that it has not simply been carried over to a new implement? Inversely, Mathieu de Dombasle called the implement which he had invented a *charrue,* although, since it had no wheels, it was actually an *araire.*

Yet this attachment to inherited names appears much stronger as soon as we consider realities of a less material order. That is because the transformations in such cases almost always take place too slowly to be perceptible to the very men affected by them. They feel no need to change the label, because the change of content escapes them. The Latin word *servus,* which has given the word *serf* to the French language, has come down through the centuries. But it has done so at the expense of so many successive alterations in the conditions so designated, that the differences between the *servus* of ancient Rome and the *serf* of the France of St. Louis far outnumber the similarities. Hence, historians have generally chosen to reserve "serf" for the Middle Ages. For antiquity, they say "slave." In other words, under the circumstances, they prefer the equivalent to the carbon copy. They do so not without a sacrifice of propriety to exactitude; for the term which they thereby transplant into a Roman environment did not come into existence until about the year 1000, to describe the markets of human flesh where captive Slavs seemed to provide the very model of a complete subjection which had become entirely unknown to the indigenous serfs of the west. The device is useful, as long as we confine ourselves to extremes. In the intervening gap, where must the slave give way to the serf? It is the eternal sophism of the shock of corn. At any rate, in order to do justice to the facts themselves, we are here forced to substitute for the language of the past a nomenclature which, if it is not strictly invented, is at least reshaped and shifted about.

Conversely, moreover, the names sometimes vary according to time or place, independently of any variation in the things themselves.

Sometimes, there are causes, peculiar to the evolution of language, which may lead to the obliteration of the word without the object or the action being in the least affected. For linguistic facts have their own coefficient of resistance or of malleability. By establishing the disappearance from the Romance languages of the Latin verb *emere* (to buy) and its replacement by other verbs of very different origins—*acheter*, *comprar*, etc.—a scholar once thought himself able to prove the most extensive and ingenious conclusions as to transformations in the commercial system of the societies heir to Rome. If only he had asked himself whether this indisputable fact could be treated in isolation! In the languages deriving from Latin, nothing was more common than the dropping of short-sounding words; the anemia of unstressed syllables gradually rendered them almost indistinct. It is a phenomenon of a strictly phonetic nature, and it is a laughable error to have mistaken a vagary of pronunciation for a feature of economic development.

Elsewhere, there are social conditions which resist the establishment or maintenance of a uniform vocabulary. In extremely split-up societies, like those of our Middle Ages, fundamentally identical institutions were frequently designated by very different terms, depending upon the locality. Even in our own day, rural dialects differ widely from each other, even in designating the most common objects and the most universal customs. In the central region where I write these lines, they say *village* for what, in the north, would be a *hammeau*. The *village* of the north is here a *bourg*. These verbal deviations are, in themselves, facts worth due consideration. However, should the historian conform his own terminology to them, he would not only compromise the intelligibility of his language but he would also deny himself even the work of classification, which is his first duty.

Unlike mathematics or chemistry, our science has at its disposal no system of symbols unconnected with national language. The historian speaks only with words; hence, with those of his country. If he finds realities expressed in a foreign language, he must translate. As for that, there is no serious obstacle as long as the words refer to commonplace things or actions: that ready money of the vocabulary is easily exchanged at par. On the other hand, as soon as those institutions, beliefs, and customs which play a profounder part in the peculiar life of a society make their appearance, the translation into another language, made after the likeness of a different society, becomes an enterprise fraught with dangers. For to choose an equivalent is to postulate a resemblance.

Shall we, then, in despair of the case, resign ourselves to keeping the original term, with appropriate explanations? Assuredly, that must sometimes be the proper course. In 1919, when they saw that the Weimar constitution kept the ancient name of *Reich* for the German state, certain of our publicists loudly protested: "A curious *republic* which still calls itself an *empire*!" The truth is not only that *Reich* does not, of itself, imply the idea of an emperor, but that, by its association with a political history constantly oscillating between particularism and unity, the word has a ring far too specifically German to suffer the least attempt at translation into a language which reflects an entirely different national past.

But such mechanical adoption of foreign words, obviously the easiest solution, cannot be made a general rule. Even putting aside any concern for propriety of language, it would still be annoying to see historians encumbering their observations with foreign expressions like those authors of rustic novels who, by their use of provincialisms, slip into a jargon which neither town nor country would recognize as its own. To renounce any attempt at equivalence is often to do injury to reality itself. A custom which derives, I believe, from the eighteenth century permits the use of the French word *serf*, or of closely related words in other Western languages, to designate the *Krepostnoi* of tsarist Russia. A more unfortunate comparison would be difficult to imagine. In Russia there was a system of attachment to the land gradually transformed into true slavery; with us, a form of personal dependence which, despite its severity, was very far from treating man as a thing deprived of all rights: the so-called Russian serfdom had almost nothing in common with our medieval serfdom. Simply to say "Krepostnoi," however, will hardly help our case. For, in Rumania, in Hungary, in Poland, and even in eastern Germany, there have been types of peasant subjection closely related to that established in Russia. Must we speak Rumanian, Hungarian, Polish, German, and Russian by turns? Once more, we should miss the essential point, which is to map the underlying connections between the facts by expressing them with an accurate nomenclature.

The label has been badly chosen. But that does not obviate the necessity of a common label, and one which is, therefore, superimposed upon national words, instead of merely copying them. Here again, passivity is forbidden.

Numerous societies have practiced what may be called a hierarchic bilingualism. Two languages are side by side, the one popular, the other learned. What is generally thought and spoken in the first is written, either exclusively or by preference, in the second. Thus, from the eleventh to the seventeenth century the Abyssinians wrote Gueze, but spoke Amharic. Thus, the Evangelists reported in Greek, which was then the great language of Eastern culture, conversations which we must assume to have been originally exchanged in Aramaic. Thus, more recently, the Middle Ages for long conducted its administration and wrote its narratives only in Latin. Inherited from dead or borrowed from foreign civilizations, these languages of the lettered, the priests, and the scribes came of necessity to express a great many realities for which they had not originally been framed. They succeeded in this only with the help of a whole system of transpositions, which were inevitably rather awkward.

Now—material evidences excepted—it is by means

of these writings that we come to know a society. Hence, those societies in which such a dualism of languages prevails appear to us in many of their principal characteristics only through a sort of veil. Sometimes, moreover, a supplementary screen intervenes. The great land-register instituted by William the Conqueror, the Doomsday Book, was the work of clerks of Normandy or Maine. Not only did they describe in Latin institutions which were peculiarly English, but they had first thought them over in French. When the historian runs into this sort of nomenclature by substitution, he has no other recourse than to do the work over in reverse. If the corresponding terms were suitably chosen and, above all, consistently applied, the task will be relatively easy. It will not be very difficult to recognize the counts of real life behind the "consuls" of the chroniclers. Unfortunately, there are less favorable cases to be met with. What was the *colonus* of our eleventh and twelfth century charters? It is a meaningless question. With no derivative in the language of the people, because it had ceased to apply to any living idea, the word represented a mere trick of translation used by the notaries to describe, in fine classic Latin, a whole series of very different judicial and economic conditions.

At any rate, this opposition of two necessarily different languages actually typifies only an extreme instance of contrasts common to all societies. Even within the most unified nations, such as ours, each little professional community, each group distinguished by virtue of its culture or wealth, has its own characteristic form of expression. Now, not all groups write, or write as much or have as much chance of passing their writings down to posterity. Everyone knows that the official reports of a judicial examination seldom reproduce the words just as they were spoken; almost spontaneously, the clerk of the court orders, clarifies, restores the syntax, and weeds out the words which he has judged too vulgar. The civilizations of the past have also had their clerks; it is the voice of chroniclers and, especially, jurists which has come through to us before all others. We must beware of forgetting that the words which they used, and the classifications which they suggested by these words, were the result of a learned elaboration often unduly influenced by tradition. What a shock it might be if, instead of poring laboriously over the jumbled—and probably artificial—terminology of the Carolingian manorial scrolls and capitularies, we were able to take a walk through a village of that time, overhearing the peasants discussing their status amongst themselves, or the seigneurs describing that of their dependents. Doubtless this description of daily usage would fail of itself to give us a total picture of life, for the attempts at expression and, hence, at interpretation by scholars and men of the law also embody really effective forces; but it would at least give us the underlying feeling. What an education it would be—whether as to the God of yesterday or today—were we able to hear the true prayers on the lips of the humble! Assuming, of course, that they themselves knew how to express the impulses of their hearts without mutilating them.

For there, in the last analysis, is the great obstacle. Nothing is more difficult for us than self-expression. But we experience scarcely less difficulty in finding names, free from both ambiguity and false precision, to express the fluid social realities in which we have our very being. The most usual terms are never more than approximations. These include even the religious terms which one might easily imagine to have a precise meaning. If you examine the religious situation of France, you will see how many subtle distinctions a learned man like M. Le Bras is today forced to substitute for that oversimplified label: "Catholic." This is food for thought for those historians who, from atop the eminence of their belief (sometimes, and perhaps more frequently, of their unbelief) are inflexibly dogmatic about the Catholicism of an Erasmus. Certain other very vital realities have failed to find suitable words. A laborer in our day finds it easy to speak of his class consciousness, even though it may be rather deficient. I doubt that this sentiment of conscious and aroused solidarity has ever manifested itself with more force or clarity than among the agricultural laborers of northern France at the end of the Ancien Régime; various petitions, certain memorials of 1789 have preserved its poignant echoes for us. Nevertheless, their sentiment could not then have been named, because there was still no name for it.

. . .

To sum it all up in a word, the vocabulary of documents is, in its way, only another form of evidence. It is, no doubt, an extremely valuable one, but, like all evidences, imperfect and hence subject to criticism. Each significant term, each characteristic turn of style becomes a true component of knowledge—but not until it has been placed in its context, related to the usage of the epoch, of the society or of the author; and above all, if it is a survival of ancient date, secured from the ever-present danger of an anachronistic misinterpretation. Royal unction in the twelfth century was treated as a sacrament, and the term "sacrament" was assuredly fraught with significance, but it lacked, at that time, the far greater weight which theology would assign to it today, having become more inflexible in its definitions and, consequently, in its vocabulary. The advent of the name is always a great event even though the thing named has preceded it; for it signifies the decisive moment of conscious awareness. What a forward stride was taken the day the initiates of a new faith first called themselves Christians! Certain of our elders, like Fustel de Coulanges, have given us admirable examples of this study of meanings, of this "historical semantics." Since their time, the progress of linguistics has further sharpened the tool. May young scholars never grow weary of handling it and, especially, of extending its use into the most recent times, which, in this regard, are much the least well explored.

Certainly, in spite of everything, the names, however

imperfect their over-all accuracy, have far too strong a grip upon reality ever to permit us to describe a society without making a considerable use of its words, duly explained and interpreted. We shall not imitate those everlasting translators of the Middle Ages. We shall say "counts" where it is a question of counts, and "consuls" where ancient Rome is the setting. Great progress was made in the understanding of Hellenic religions as soon as Zeus had definitely banished Jupiter from the lips of scholars. But this practice is particularly applicable to institutional, technological, or religious detail. To consider that the nomenclature of the documents was perfectly capable of determining our own would, in short, be tantamount to admitting that they had provided us with a ready-made analysis. Were that the case, history would have little left to do. Happily, for our sake, it is not. That is why we are forced to seek elsewhere for the broad framework of our classification.

To provide it, we already have at our disposal a whole lexicon which seeks to transcend the connotations of any particular period. Elaborated without predetermined plan by the successive modifications of several generations of historians, it brings together elements of very diverse date and origin. "Feudal" and "feudalism" were originally legal jargon, taken over from the courts of the eighteenth century by Boulainvilliers, and then by Montesquieu, to become the rather awkward labels for a type of social structure which was itself rather ill-defined. "Capital" was a usurer's and accountant's word whose meaning the early economists greatly expanded. "Capitalist" is a remnant of the language of speculators in the earliest European stock-exchanges. But "capitalism," which today occupies a far more considerable place in our classics, is altogether new: its ending shows its origin—*Kapitalismus*. "Revolution" has changed its former astrological associations for a very human meaning; in the heavens, it was and still is a regular motion, forever turning back upon itself; on earth, a sharp crisis always aimed straight ahead. "Proletariat" is a word of antique style, like the men of '89 who first made its fortune, following Rousseau: but Marx, following Babeuf, has set his stamp on it forever. The very savages of America have given us "totem," and those of Oceania, "taboo": ethnographic adaptations before which the classicism of certain historians still hesitates.

Neither this variety of origins, nor these deviations of meaning are an inconvenience. A word is valued much less for its etymology than for the use to which it is put. If "capitalism," even in its broadest application, is far from embracing all those economic systems in which the capital of moneylenders has played a role; if "feudal" currently serves to characterize societies in which the fief was certainly not the most significant feature, that in no way contradicts the universal practice of all sciences, which as soon as they are no longer content with pure algebraic symbols are obliged to draw upon the confused vocabulary of daily life. Are we scandalized that the physicist persists in using the term "atom," meaning indivisible, for what is actually the object of his most daring dissections?

Much more dangerous are those emotional overtones with which so many of these words are charged as they come to us. Strong feeling is seldom favorable to precision of language.

Even among historians, custom tends to confuse the two expressions, "feudal system" and "seigneurial system," in the most troublesome manner. This is arbitrarily to equate the complex of dependent ties characteristic of a warrior aristocracy with a type of peasant subjection which not only was very different by nature but had arisen very much earlier, lasted much longer, and was far more widespread throughout the world.

The misunderstanding dates back to the eighteenth century. At that time, vassalage and the fief still existed, but only as a legal form which had been virtually devoid of meaning for several centuries. The seigneury, on the other hand, although descended from the same past, remained very much alive. The political writers had made no distinctions within this heritage. It was not only that they misunderstood it. For the most part, they did not consider it dispassionately. They detested it for its anachronisms and, even more, for the oppressive forces which it persistently embodied. A common condemnation enveloped the whole. Then, at the same time and under a single name, the Revolution abolished the seigneury along with those institutions which were properly feudal. All that remained was a memory, but a persistent one, which descriptions of the strife of the last days painted in vivid colors. Henceforth, the confusion was established. Born out of passion, it continued ever ready to be spread under the stimulus of new passions. Even today, are we entirely dispassionate when we speak of industrial or financial "feudalisms"? In the background there is always a reflection of the firing of châteaux during the burning summer of '89.

Now, unfortunately, such is the fate of a great many of our words. They continue to live among us the unquiet life of public disputation. It is not the historians who nowadays harangue us to consider capitalism and communism as identical. Our symbols are variable according to time or place; they become coefficients of emotivity leading to further equivocation. The reactionaries of 1815 hid their faces in horror at the very name of revolution. Those of 1940 used it to camouflage their *coup d'état.*

However, let us assume that our vocabulary had ultimately arrived at impassiveness. Even the most intellectual of languages have their pitfalls. Certainly, we here feel not the slightest temptation to republish those "nominalist pleasantries" of which Robert Simiand once observed, with good reason, that the sciences of man had a kind of monopoly. What law denies us those facilities of language which are indispensable for any rational knowledge? If, for example, we speak of the factory system, we by no means create an entity thereby. We merely group facts, as concrete as we could wish, under an expressive name. The similitude of these facts, which the name quite properly seeks to signify, is itself a reality. In themselves, therefore, these terms are entirely legitimate. Their true danger derives from their very convenience. If ill-chosen or too mechanically applied, the symbol (which was there only to assist in the analysis) ends by dispensing with analysis. Thereby, it promotes anachronism: the most unpardonable of sins in a time-science.

Medieval societies distinguished two principal human conditions: there were men who were free, others who were not considered to be so. But the idea of liberty is one which each epoch reshapes to its own liking. Therefore, certain historians nowadays have judged that, in the allegedly normal, which is to say, in their own acceptation of the word, the unfree men of the Middle Ages had been badly designated. They were, they say, "half-free." As a word invented without any textual authority, this intruder would be awkward in any case. Unfortunately, it is worse than that. As a nearly inevitable consequence, such false precision seems to have made superfluous any extensive research on the line between liberty and servitude, as these civilizations understood the idea: a line which was often uncertain and even variable according to the bias of the time or of the class, but one of whose essential characteristics was precisely that of having never allowed that marginal zone which the name of half-liberty suggests with such tiresome persistence. A nomenclature which is thrust upon the past will always end by distorting it, whether by design or simply as a consequence of equating its categories with our own, raised, for the moment, to the level of the eternal. There is no reasonable attitude toward such labels except to eliminate them.

"Capitalism" has been a useful word. Doubtless, it will again become so when we have succeeded in cleansing it of those ambiguities with which its passage into common use has increasingly burdened it. At the moment, carelessly applied to the most diverse civilizations, it almost inevitably results in concealing their original features. Was the economic system of the sixteenth century "capitalist"? Perhaps. However, consider that sort of universal discovery of the profit motive which was then trickling from the top of society to the bottom, catching up the shopkeeper or village notary as well as the great banker of Augsburg or Lyons; observe that the emphasis was placed upon loans or commercial speculations far earlier than upon the organization of production: how different then is this "capitalism" of the Renaissance, in its human structure, from the far more hierarchically organized system of modern manufacturing or the St. Simonian system of the era of the Industrial Revolution. Which, in its turn . . .

In any case, one very simple observation should suffice to put us on our guard. If we think of capitalism, no longer as the capitalism of one definite period, but capitalism in and of itself, Capitalism with a capital

"C," what date shall we assign to its appearance? The twelfth century in Italy? The thirteenth in Flanders? At the time of the Fuggers and the exchange at Antwerp? The eighteenth century, or even the nineteenth? There are as many birth-certificates as there are historians. Indeed, they are almost as numerous as for that bourgeoisie whose rise to power is so celebrated in our textbooks, and which is variously stated, for the edification of schoolboys, to have occurred in the reign of Philip the Fair, or in that of Louis XIV, unless it was in 1789, or in 1830. Could it be, after all, that it was not the same bourgeoisie? Or not the same capitalism?

And here, I believe, we strike the root of the matter. We are reminded of the neat phrase of Fontenelle: "Leibniz," he remarked, "laid down exact definitions, which deprived him of the agreeable liberty to misuse his terms upon occasion." Agreeable perhaps; certainly dangerous. It is a liberty with which we are all too familiar. The historian seldom defines. He might well consider this an unnecessary precaution, if he were borrowing from a usage which was itself strictly defined. Since such is not the case, almost his only guide, even in the use of his key words, is personal instinct. He arbitrarily expands, restricts, distorts the meanings —without warning his reader; without always fully realizing it himself. What of the "feudalisms" throughout the world from China to the Greece of the beautifully greaved Achæans? For the most part, they bear scarcely any resemblance to each other. That is because nearly every historian understands the word as he pleases.

However, even if we do define, it is usually every man for himself. Nothing is more significant than the case of an economic analyst as penetrating as John Maynard Keynes. There is hardly one of his books in which he does not, from the beginning, expropriate terms, usually pretty well established, in order to decree entirely new meanings for them, meanings which sometimes vary from work to work, but, in any case, intentionally depart from common usage. Curious whim of the sciences of man, which, after long being ranked among the "*Belles-lettres,*" seem still to preserve something of the stubborn individualism of art! Can we imagine a chemist saying: "Two elements are necessary to make a molecule of water: two atoms of one, one of the other; in *my* vocabulary, the former is to be called oxygen and the latter, hydrogen"? However well defined, the private languages of historians will never, laid side by side, constitute the language of history.

To tell the truth, some better-planned efforts have been attempted here and there, by groups of specialists (linguists, ethnographers, geographers) whom the relative youth of their disciplines seems to have protected from the worst corporate habits. The task has also been undertaken for history as a whole by the Center of Synthesis, always alert to render services and provide examples. We should expect a great deal from them, but even more from a general diffusion of good will.

No doubt the day will come when a series of understandings will permit us to clarify nomenclature, and then to define it progressively. Even then, the individuality of the scholar will, as always, be reflected in his choice of words, unless he is content to limp along from one date to the next, like a mere writer of annals.

The great epochs were marked out by the dominations of conquering peoples who successively destroyed each other. Thus, the collective memory of the Middle Ages subsisted almost entirely upon the Biblical myth of the Four Empires: Assyrian, Persian, Greek, and Roman. An awkward scheme, if ever there was one. Not only did it, by compliance with the sacred text, prolong the illusion of a fictitious Roman unity but, by a curious paradox for a Christian society—as it must appear to any historian today—it made the Passion seem a less notable stage in the progress of humanity than the victories of celebrated spoilers of provinces. Within each nation, the succession of kings furnished the boundaries for the smaller divisions.

These habits have proven remarkably tenacious. *L'histoire de France,* a faithful mirror of the French school about 1900, still proceeds by stumbling from reign to reign; at each prince's death, which it narrates with all the detail which is reserved for great events, it calls a halt. When there are no longer any kings, there are governmental regimes which are also, fortunately, mortal: hence their revolutions serve as landmarks. More recently, there has been an important collection of textbooks which segments the course of modern history according to national "preponderances"—the sugar-coated equivalents of the "empires" of former times. It is hardly necessary to say that the Spanish, French, or English "hegemonies" are diplomatic and military by nature. All else one arrays as one can.

Yet long ago the eighteenth century made its protest heard. "It seems," wrote Voltaire, "that, for fourteen hundred years, there have been none but kings, ministers, and generals in the Gauls." As a consequence, there gradually appeared new divisions which, free from the imperialist or monarchical obsession, could be ordered according to profounder phenomena. As we have seen, "feudalism," as the name of a period as well as of a social system, dates from this time. But the career of the term "Middle Ages" is the most instructive of all.

In its remote origin, it was itself medieval. It belonged to the vocabulary of that semi-heretical prophecy which, from the thirteenth century especially, had captivated so many troubled spirits. The Incarnation had put an end to the Old Law. It had not yet established the Kingdom of God. Striving toward that blessed day, the present time was, therefore, only an intermediate age: a *medium ævum*. Then, with the early humanists, to whom that mystical language was apparently still familiar, the idea was misappropriated for more profane realities. In a sense, the reign of the Spirit had arrived. It was that "restoration" of thought and of letters which was then making such a vivid impression upon the best minds: such, for example, as Rabelais and Ronsard. The "Middle Age" was now closed, having represented only a prolonged waiting between a fruitful Antiquity and a new Revelation. Thus understood, the expression had a shadowy existence for several generations, confined, no doubt, to a few erudite circles. It was, it is believed, just at the close of the seventeenth century that a German, an unassuming writer of manuals, Christopher Keller, in a work of general history, thought of labeling as the "Middle Age" the whole period of more than a thousand years which extended from the Invasions to the Renaissance. By whatever channels it was introduced, the usage became firmly established in European and especially in French historiography about the time of Guizot and Michelet.

Voltaire had not known of it: "You wish ultimately to overcome the disgust you feel at Modern history since the decline of the Roman Empire." We here recognize the first sentence of the *Essai sur les Mœurs.* Nevertheless, there can be no question that the true sense of the *Essai,* which was so influential upon the succeeding generations, was responsible for the success of the term "Middle Age," as well as that of its almost inevitable counterpart, "Renaissance." Although the latter had been current in the vocabulary of the history of the fine arts, as a common noun, with the necessary addition of a complement (as in "the renaissance of the arts or letters under Leo X or Francis I"), it was not much before Michelet that, along with the capital letter, it won the distinction of being used by itself to designate the entire period. For both periods the idea is the same. Formerly, battles, court politics, the rise or fall of great dynasties had furnished the general framework within which art, literature, and the sciences were fitted more or less badly. Now it was to be the reverse. It is the most refined manifestations of the human spirit which, by their varying progress, have set the tone of the historical epochs. There is no idea which bears the Voltairian stamp more clearly than this.

But a serious weakness invalidated this classification of Middle Ages and Renaissance: the distinguishing feature also implied a judgment. "Europe, squeezed between sacerdotal tyranny and military despotism, waits amidst blood and tears for the moment when the new enlightenment will enable it to rise again to liberty, humanity, and virtue." Thus Condorcet described the period to which unanimous consent was soon to assign the name of Middle Age. But as soon as we no longer believe in that "night," as soon as we no longer picture as a uniformly barren waste the centuries which were so rich in the fields of technical invention, art, feeling, and religious reflection, which saw the first expansion of the European economy and the beginning of European nationalism, what reason can we have for confusing under one fallacious generalization the Gaul of Clovis with the France of Philip the Fair, Alcuin with St. Thomas or Ockham, the animalistic "barbarian" jewelry with the statues of Chartres, the cramped towns of Carolingian times with the flourishing bourgeoisie of Genoa, Bruges, or Lübeck. In truth, the term "Middle Age" has no more than a humble pedagogical function, as a debatable convenience for school curriculums, or as a label for erudite techniques whose scope is moreover ill-defined by the traditional dates. A medievalist is a man who knows how to read old scripts, to criticize a charter, to understand Old French. Unquestionably, that is something. It is certainly not enough to satisfy a real science in its search for accurate periodization.

Into the confusion of our chronological classifications there has stolen a fashion which is rather recent, I believe, but is all the more insidious because it has no rational basis. We tend to count by centuries.

For long disassociated with any exact enumeration of years, this word also originally had its mystic overtones—its accents of the *Fourth Eclogue* or of the *Dies Iræ*.[1] Perhaps these had not completely died away at the time when history, with no great concern for numerical precision, lingered complacently over the "century of Pericles," or that of "Louis XIV." But our language has become more rigorously mathematical. We no longer name ages after their heroes. We very prudently number them in sequence every hundred

[1] [*Translator's note: It seems necessary to point out that the French for "century" is* siècle, *which also means "age" or "era" or "temporal world," in which sense the Latin* sæculum *occurs in Vergil's* Fourth Eclogue *and in the medieval* Dies Iræ.]

years, starting from a point fixed, once and for all, at the year 1 of the Christian era. The art of the thirteenth century, the philosophy of the eighteenth, the "stupid nineteenth": these faces in arithmetical masks haunt the pages of our books. Which of us will boast of having never fallen prey to the lures of their apparent convenience?

Unfortunately, no law of history enjoins that only those years whose dates end with the figures "01" coincide with the critical points of human evolution. Whence there derive some curious distortions of meaning. "It is well known that the eighteenth century begins in 1715 and ends in 1789." Not long ago I read this sentence in a student's paper. Whether it was naïve or sly I do not know. In any case, it exposed certain singularities of the usage rather neatly. But, were it a question of the philosophical eighteenth century, we might certainly prefer to say that it began well before 1701: the *Histoire des Oracles* appeared in 1687, and Bayle's *Dictionnaire* in 1697. The worst of it is that since the name, as always, carries the idea along with it, these false labels end by misrepresenting the merchandise. The medievalists speak of the "Renaissance of the twelfth century." Certainly, there was then a great intellectual movement. However, if this is what we call it, we are too apt to forget that it actually began about 1060, and hence to miss certain essential connections. In a word, we appear to assign an arbitrarily chosen and strictly pendulumlike rhythm to realities to which such regularity is entirely alien. It is an impossible task. Naturally, we do very badly at it. We must look for something better.

The long and the short of it is that, as long as we confine ourselves to studying sequences or phenomena in time, the problem is simple. We should look to the phenomena themselves for their proper periods. A religious history of the reign of Philip Augustus? An economic history of the reign of Louis XV? Why not: "Journal of what happened in my laboratory during the second presidency of Grévy," by Louis Pasteur? Or, inversely: "Diplomatic history of Europe from Newton to Einstein"?

Of course, we readily understand the potential charms of divisions regularly arranged according to empires, kings, or political regimes. Not only do they have the prestige which a long tradition associates with the exercise of power, "with those deeds," as Machiavelli puts it, "which have the air of grandeur proper to acts of government or of the state"; but an accession, a revolution, has its chronological position determined to a year and even to a day. Now, the scholar loves close dating. He finds it both an appeasement to his instinctive horror of the vague and a great comfort to the conscience. He wants to have read and to have checked everything which concerns his subject. How much easier this will be if, standing before each file of archives with his calendar in his hand, he can divide them into categories: before, during, and after!

However, let us beware of worshipping the idol of

false precision. The most precise measurement is not necessarily the one which refers to the smallest unit of time—in which case, we should have to prefer not only a year to a decade, but also a second to a day—it is the one which is best adapted to the nature of the events. Now, each type of phenomenon has its own particular dimension of measurement and, so to speak, its own specific decimal. Metamorphoses of social structure, economy, beliefs, or mental attitude cannot conform to an overly precise chronology without distortion. When I write that a very profound change, marked simultaneously by the first large-scale imports of overseas wheat and by the first great expansion of German and American industry, took place in the economy of the West between about 1875 and 1885, I make use of the nearest approximation permitted by this kind of fact. A date pretending to be more exact would falsify the truth. Even in statistics a decennial average is, in itself, no more crude than an annual or weekly average. It merely expresses another aspect of reality.

Moreover, it is by no means impossible *a priori* that phases of phenomena of a seemingly very different order may overlap in experience. Is it true that the advent of the Second Empire ushered in a new economic era in France? Was Sombart right in identifying the rise of capitalism with that of the Protestant spirit? Was M. Thierry-Maulnier right when he found in democracy "the political expression" of this same capitalism (although not, I fear, quite the same capitalism)? However dubious such coincidences may seem to us, we have no right to reject them with closed minds. We simply must not postulate such connections in advance. Certainly, the tides are related to the successive phases of the moon. In order to know this, however, it was first necessary to determine the periods of the tides and those of the moon, quite apart from one another.

When, on the other hand, we consider the evolution of society as a whole, can we characterize its successive stages? The problem is to find the dominant note. We can here only suggest the ways in which a classification might be worked out. Let us not forget that history is a science still in travail.

Men who are born into the same social environment about the same time necessarily come under analogous influences, particularly in their formative years. Experience proves that, by comparison with either considerably older or considerably younger groups, their behavior reveals certain distinctive characteristics which are ordinarily very clear. This is true even of their bitterest disagreements. To be excited by the same dispute even on opposing sides, is still to be alike. This common stamp, deriving from common age, is what makes a generation.

Society, it is true, is not a single thing. It is split up into different social classes, in which the generations do not always overlap. Do the forces acting upon a young worker necessarily operate, at least with equal intensity, upon a young peasant? Add to this that, even in the best-knit civilizations, the currents of dissemination are slow. My father, born in Strassburg in 1848, used to say: "We were romantics in the Provinces during my adolescence, when Paris had ceased to be so." Often, however, as in this case, the contrast is no more than a lag. Consequently, when we speak of such and such a generation in France, for example, we call forth a complex and, sometimes, even a contradictory idea—but one in which it is natural to retain the really dominant elements.

Despite the Pythagorean dreams of certain authors, it is obvious that the periodicity of the generations is by no means regular. As the rhythm of social change is more or less rapid, the limits contract or expand. There are, in history, some generations which are long and some which are short. Only observation enables us to perceive the points at which the curve changes its direction. At my university the dates of enrollment made it easy to note one such turning-point. I early found that I was, in many respects, closer to the classes that had graduated before me than to those which came almost immediately after me. My classmates and I considered ourselves as the last of the generation of the Dreyfus Affair. The experience of life has not contradicted this impression.

It is inevitable for the generations to permeate each other, for individuals do not always react in the same way to the same influences. Among our children, it is today fairly easy to distinguish, mainly according to ages, between the war and the postwar generations. Always with this one reservation: in those who have not reached late adolescence, but are past early childhood, the sensitivity to present events varies a great deal according to personal temperament; the most precocious will be truly "of the war"; the others will be left on the opposite bank.

Accordingly, like any concept which seeks to express, without distortion, the affairs of man, the notion of one generation is very elastic. It corresponds to realities which we feel to be very concrete. It has long been used instinctively by those disciplines whose nature is particularly hostile to the old divisions by reigns or governments—such as the history of thought or of artistic forces. Increasingly, it seems destined to provide a first step toward a rational analysis of human change.

But a generation represents only a relatively short phase. Longer phases are called civilizations.

Thanks to Lucien Febvre, we are well acquainted with the history of the word, which is obviously inseparable from that of the idea. Only slowly has the idea been disentangled—or, more precisely, disassociated—from value judgment. We still speak (although, alas, with less assurance than our elders) of civilization in itself, of civilization as an ideal, and of the difficult ascent of mankind toward its noble tranquillity; but we speak also of civilizations in the plural and merely as realities. From this point, we admit that there may be, if I may venture to say so, civilizations of people who are not civilized. That is because we have come to recognize that within any society, whatever its nature, everything is mutually controlled and connected: the political and social structure, the economy, the beliefs, the most rudimentary as well as the subtlest manifestations of the mind. What shall we call this complex, "in the heart of which," as Guizot once wrote, "all the forces of its existence come together"? Created by the eighteenth century to express an absolute good, the word "civilization," without losing its former meaning, has conformed naturally to this new sense of fact, in proportion as the sciences of man have become more relativist. What was formerly its sole meaning it now preserves as an echo of human sympathy, whose value is not to be overlooked.

The antitheses of civilizations appeared clearly as soon as the contrasting features of exotic lands were noted. Will any one deny that there is a Chinese civilization today, or that it differs greatly from the European? But, even in the same region, the major emphases of the social complex may be more or less abruptly modified. When such a transformation has taken place, we say that one civilization succeeds another. Sometimes there is an external shock, ordinarily accompanied by the introduction of new human elements, such as between the Roman Empire and the societies of the high Middle Ages. Sometimes, on the other hand, there is simply internal change. Everyone will agree that the civilization of the Renaissance is no longer ours, despite the fact that we have derived such a liberal inheritance from it. These varying tonalities are, no doubt, difficult to express. They cannot be expressed by summary labels. The convenience of "ism" words (*Typismus, Konventionalismus*) ruined even such an intelligent attempt at evolutionary description as Karl Lamprecht's *History of Germany*. The same error was earlier made by Taine, in whose writings we are astonished nowadays by the almost personal reality of the "dominant conception." Nevertheless, the fact that certain attempts may have miscarried does not justify abandoning the effort. It is the business of research to introduce more accuracy and exactness into these distinctions.

To summarize, human time will never conform to the implacable uniformity or fixed divisions of clock time. Reality demands that its measurements be suited to the variability of its rhythm, and that its boundaries have wide marginal zones. It is only by this plasticity that history can hope to adapt its classifications, as Bergson put it, "to the very contours of reality": which is properly the ultimate aim of any science.

CHAPTER V

HISTORICAL CAUSATION

In vain positivism claimed to eliminate the idea of cause from science. Whether he likes it or not, every physicist, every biologist thinks in terms of "why" and "because." The historian cannot escape this common law of the mind. Some, like Michelet, connect matters in a great "living movement," rather than give an explanation in logical form; others parade their apparatus of inductions and hypotheses; the genetic link is present throughout. But from the fact that establishment of relations of cause and effect constitutes an instinctive need of our understanding, it does not follow that the search can be left to instinct. If the metaphysics of causality is here beyond our horizon, the use of the causal relationship as a tool of historical knowledge indisputably demands a conscious critical treatment.

Let us suppose that a man is walking along a mountain path. He trips and falls off a precipice. For this accident to happen, the combination of a great number of determining elements was necessary, such as, among others, the existence of gravity; a terrain resulting from protracted geological changes; the laying out of a path for the purpose, let us say, of connecting a village with its summer pastures. It would, therefore, be perfectly legitimate to say that, were the laws of celestial mechanics different, had the evolution of the earth been otherwise, were alpine economy not founded upon the seasonal migration of flocks, the fall would not have happened. Nevertheless, should we inquire as to the cause, everyone would answer: "A misstep." It is not that this antecedent was most necessary to the occurrence of the event. Many others were just as necessary. But it was distinguished from all the rest by several very striking characteristics: it occurred last; it was the least permanent, the most exceptional in the general order of things; finally, by virtue of this greater particularity, it seems the antecedent which could have been most easily avoided. For these reasons, it appears to have exerted a more direct influence upon the result, and we scarcely can avoid the feeling that it was really the sole cause of it. From the viewpoint of common sense, which has always been reluctant to rid itself of a certain anthropomorphism in speaking of cause, this last-minute component, this specific and unexpected component, is a little like the artist who gives form to a plastic material which is already completely prepared.

Historical reasoning in contemporary practice does not differ in its procedure. However necessary they may be, the most constant and general antecedents remain merely implicit. What military historian would dream of ranking among the causes of a victory that gravitation which accounts for the trajectory of the shells, or the physiological organization of the human body without which the projectiles would have no fatal consequences? More specific antecedents, if they have a certain permanence, form what is called, for convenience, "the conditions." The most specific, the one which somehow represents the differentiating element in the compound of generative influences, is accorded the name of cause. We will say, for example, that the inflation of Law's time was the cause of the over-all rise of prices. The existence in France of a homogeneous and well-knit economic milieu would be only a condition. For that ease of circulation which, by distributing notes on all sides, simply made possible the rise, both preceded the inflation and outlasted it.

There can be no doubt that there is a faithful principle of research in this discrimination. What is the use of dwelling upon nearly universal antecedents? They are common to too many phenomena to deserve a special niche in the genealogy of any of them. I am well aware, from the outset, that there would be no fire if the air contained no oxygen: what interests me, what demands and justifies an attempt at discovery, is to determine how the fire started. The laws of trajectories are as valid for defeat as for victory: they explain both; therefore, they are useless as a proper explanation for either.

However, a graduated classification of causes, which

is really only an intellectual convenience, cannot safely be elevated to an absolute. Reality offers us a nearly infinite number of lines of force which all converge together upon the same phenomenon. The choice we make among them may well be founded upon characteristics which, in practice, fully merit our attention; but it is always a choice. Notably, there is something extremely arbitrary in the idea of a cause *par excellence*, as opposed to mere "conditions." Even Simiand, who was so possessed by the idea of precision, and who had begun with an attempt (a vain one, I believe) for stricter definitions, seems to have ended by recognizing the entirely relative character of such distinctions. "For a doctor," he wrote, "the cause of an epidemic would be the multiplication of a microbe and its conditions the dirt and ill health occasioned by poverty; for the sociologist and the philanthropist, poverty would be the cause, and the biological factors, the condition." This is in all honesty to acknowledge the subordination of the perspective to the peculiar angle of the inquiry. Moreover, let us take care: in history, the fetish of single cause is all too often only the insidious form of search for the responsible person—hence a value judgment. The judge expresses it as: "Who is right, and who is wrong?" The scholar is content to ask: "Why?" and he accepts the fact that the answer may not be simple. Whether as a prejudice of common sense, a postulate of logicians, or a habit of prosecuting attorneys, the monism of cause can be, for history, only an impediment. History seeks for causal wave-trains and is not afraid, since life shows them to be so, to find them multiple.

Historical facts are, in essence, psychological facts. Normally, therefore, they find their antecedents in other psychological facts. To be sure, human destinies are placed in the physical world and suffer the consequence thereof. Even where the intrusion of these external forces seems most brutal, however, their action is weakened or intensified by man and his mind. The virus of the Black Death was the prime cause of the depopulation of Europe. But the epidemic spread so rapidly only by virtue of certain social—and, therefore, in their underlying nature, mental—conditions, and its moral effects are to be explained only by the peculiar propensities of collective sensibility.

However, there can be no psychology which confines itself to pure consciousness. To read certain books of history, one might think mankind made up entirely of logical wills whose reasons for acting would never hold the slightest mystery for them. In view of the actual state of investigation into the life of the mind and its obscure depths, this is a further proof of the everlasting difficulty which the sciences experience in trying to remain contemporaneous with each other. Moreover, it is to repeat in exaggerated form the often denounced error of an obsolete economic theory. *Homo œconomicus* was an empty shadow, not only because he was supposedly preoccupied by self-interest; the worst illusion consisted in imagining that he could form so clear an idea of his interests. Napoleon once said: "There is nothing so rare as a plan." Does anyone consider that the oppressive moral atmosphere in which we are currently plunged comes only from the rational part of our minds? We should seriously misrepresent the problem of causes in history if we always and everywhere reduced them to a problem of motive.

Moreover, what a curious contradiction there is in the successive attitudes of so many historians: when it is a question of ascertaining whether or not some human act has really taken place, they cannot be sufficiently painstaking. If they proceed to the reasons for that act, they are content with the merest appearance, ordinarily founded upon one of those maxims of commonplace psychology which are neither more or less true than their opposites.

Two critics trained in philosophy, Georg Simmel in Germany and François Simiand in France, have amused themselves in exposing several of these *petitiones principi* for us. The Hébertists, one German historian writes, were at first in perfect accord with Robespierre because he yielded to all their desires; then they broke with him because they considered him too powerful. This, as Simmel observes in substance, is to imply the two following propositions: a favor provokes gratitude; people do not like to be dominated. Now, these two propositions are not necessarily false, to be sure. But neither are they necessarily true. For, could it not be held with equal likelihood that a too-ready submission to the will of a party might excite its contempt for your weakness rather than gratitude; and, on the other hand, have we never seen a dictator who stifled even the slightest impulse to resistance by the fear which his power inspired? A scholastic philosopher once remarked of authority that it had "a nose of wax, which bends either to left or right indiscriminately." It is the same with the pretended psychological truths of common sense.

Basically, the error is analogous to the one which inspired that pseudogeographical determinism which is today once for all discredited. Whether confronted by a phenomenon of the physical world or by a social fact, the movement of human reactions is not like clockwork always going in the same direction. Renan to the contrary notwithstanding, the desert is not necessarily "monotheistic," because the people who inhabit it do not all bring the same spirit to its scenes. Scarcity of watering-places would bring about the clustering of rural population, and abundance of water would disperse it, only if it were true that people made proximity to springs, wells, and ponds their supreme consideration. In reality they sometimes prefer, for the sake of security or co-operation, or even through mere gregariousness, to live in close groups even where every field has its spring; or inversely, as in certain regions of Sardinia, where everyone builds his dwelling in the middle of his little estate, they resign themselves to long walks for the scarce water as the price of the isolation on which they have set their hearts. Is not man himself the greatest variable in nature?

Let us not here be misled, however. In such a case, the fault is not in the explanation itself. The fault is only in accepting any explanation *a priori*. Although up to now there have been relatively few examples of it, it may well be that, under given social conditions, the distribution of water sources determines place of habitation more than any other factor. Certainly it does not determine it of necessity. It is by no means impossible that the Hébertists really did respond to those motives which their historian attributed to them. The error was in considering this hypothesis as given at the outset. It needed to be proved. Then, once this proof—which we have no right to consider as unfeasible out of prejudice—has been supplied, it still remains for us by digging deeper into the analysis to ask why, out of all the imaginable psychological attitudes, these particular ones should have imposed themselves upon the group. For, as soon as we admit that a mental or emotional reaction is not self-explanatory, we are forced in turn, whenever such a reaction occurs, to make a real effort to discover the reasons for it. In a word, in history, as elsewhere, the causes cannot be assumed. They are to be looked for. . . .